Fair Wind to Malabar

The year is 1761, France and Holland have been defeated, and the Honourable Company is looking forward to a period of consolidation in India. But two French ships of war have not surrendered and, in alliance with the Mahrattan pirates of Gheriah, threaten the whole British position in Malabar.

To Commodore Roger Kelso this threat comes when he is already plagued by personal problems. His wife, Lady Susan, whom he has sent home in disgrace, is on another ship in the convoy and, try as he may, he cannot forget her. When he leaves the convoy and Susan's ship is captured by Mahrattan pirates he acts with characteristic courage and, despite feeble protests from some members of council in Bombay, decides to take on the might of the Mahrattan empire and its French allies.

This fast-moving and exciting Kelso story, which is a direct sequel to the popular *Commodore Kelso*, will delight all readers of the series.

By the same author

JAMES DILLON WHITE

Fair Wind to Malabar

Hutchinson of London

Hutchinson & Co (Publishers) Ltd
3 Fitzroy Square, London W1P 6JD

London Melbourne Sydney Auckland
Wellington Johannesburg and agencies
throughout the world

First published 1978
© James Dillon White 1978

Set in Monotype Times
Printed in Great Britain by
The Anchor Press Ltd, and bound by
Wm Brendon & Son Ltd,
both of Tiptree, Essex

ISBN 0 09 132050 X

1

Sailing close-hauled into the wind, they beat slowly southwards and arrived off Coromandel on the seventh day of September 1761.

As they approached the coast and the sand bar which made this one of the more difficult anchorages, the crew aboard the flagship *Protector* thought hopefully of shore leave and forgot as they went about their duties that, after a brief stay in port, the monotonous tacking and wearing ship of the past week would be repeated tenfold before they reached their final destination of St Helena. In the chains the leadsman, marking their passage through the shoals, stood, handsome as a Greek god, as he swung and heaved his line and called in a deep voice, 'By the mark thirteen – by the deep nine – and a quarter eight'; the watch on deck, burnt brown as natives and looking like natives as they crouched on heels, waiting for the next call to braces, rested calloused hands on knees, shut their eyes to the sun and dreamt of cold ale and arrack and slim-waisted Indian girls; by the shrouds topmen had gathered, ready to take in canvas; the bo'sun was detailing a boat crew; forward, in the fo'c'sle, marines, waisters and loblolly boys jostled round buckets with combs and razors, hoping to hear their names called for the first shore party.

Commodore Kelso was on the quarterdeck. From his position by the weather rail, where he stood, feet astride, hands clasped behind back, he watched the slow-moving convoy and waited for Fenton to order a change to the new tack.

They had made a good landfall. To starboard the coast-line, green hills and paddy fields beyond a sandy beach, curved round the margin of a bay which was marked at the southern end by the sprawling conglomeration of ware-houses, sheds, tenements, hovels and fine houses of Madras. In the foreground, gold tinted in the morning sun, stood the East India Company fort of St George.

'Four points to starboard!'

'Four points to starboard, sir.' Sullivan, the quarter-master, anticipating Fenton's order, had already put down the wheel, so that, turning across the wind, *Protector* was swinging towards the limit of safety even as the watch scrambled to braces.

'Brace round the foreyards!'

Sweating, cursing, with bare feet sticking to the pitch which oozed and bubbled from the deck seams, the watch heaved on tackles until, with the foreyards on the new tack and the wind now on the larboard bow, the main and miz-zen yards could be braced round as *Protector* headed for the shore.

Kelso cleared his throat, ready to congratulate the captain on a good passage, but then, thinking better of it, simply called, 'Heave to, captain, if you please.' He had known Fenton long enough to make compliments un-necessary.

'Take in headsails, Mr Aitken,' Fenton called to the officer of the watch. 'Back the main tops'l. Mr Stredwick, run up the signal to heave to.'

As the midshipman raced forward to the signal locker Fenton watched, shading his eyes against the sun, and waited until the five heavily laden Indiamen had man-oeuvred into position, with the second escort vessel, the sloop *Agamemnon*, to windward, before turning to the commodore and saluting.

'Convoy in position and hove-to, sir.'

'Thank you, captain,' Kelso replied, as though he could not see for himself, even without the aid of a glass, the bluff-bowed Indiamen, the most distant of which was no more than a few cables' length away, and the tiny sloop of war.

'Will you be going ashore, sir?'

'I think not. I'd be obliged if you'd take my dispatches to the governor.'

'Aye, aye, sir. Then if you'll excuse me I'll go below to lay out my best uniform.'

Kelso nodded and watched with something like affection as Fenton hurried down the companion. How long had they been together now: ten years, or was it twelve? Which other captain would have accepted without comment or query or any sign of surprise that, arriving at one of the Company's most important posts, the commodore had decided not to go ashore?

And yet, he thought, perhaps Fenton was more perceptive than he seemed. Had he noticed, while attending to his many duties, the lone figure in white who stood day after day by the larboard taffrail of the nearest ship of the convoy, the country-built Indiaman *Cleopatra*, and, noticing, had he formed his own conclusions?

She had been there on that first day as they sailed in line down the muddy reaches of the Hooghli, she had been there at dusk as the sun set in an extravagant display of reds and purples over the dismal marshes of Cowcolli, she had been there as he came on deck at dawn the following morning. Always, like conscience or a silent reproach, she was there, seldom talking to the other passengers, it seemed, scarcely going down to eat. Was she watching now, wondering how long it would be before he called for his gig to be rowed ashore?

'Beg pardon, sir, but it's all ready on your cot.'

He turned, without quite masking his irritation, as his steward Padstow stood before him and saluted.

'What?'

'Your best uniform, sir. New stockings, or as good as new since her leddyship took 'em in hand with her needle. Shoes with buckles polished, your fancy sword – '

'I'm not going.'

'Not going!' The exclamation was out before Padstow could stop it, but then, not greatly perturbed, he assumed an expression, which Kelso knew well, of stoical acceptance. 'Then I've shaved for nothing.'

'There's no reason why you shouldn't go, in fact you'd better go. You can buy me some fruit and some green vegetables. I don't suppose you'll find any drinkable wine.'

'I'll do me best, sir,' his steward replied, with a grin. 'And if I see her leddyship – ?'

'You'll pass her by: is that understood? You'll do your best to avoid her.' He checked himself, realizing that even before Padstow, who knew most of his secrets, it would not do to show such vehemence. 'I'm sure that Lady Susan is well provided for.'

As the longboat and the gig were lowered away he could not help looking across to *Cleopatra* where, as on *Protector*, some of the crew were preparing to go ashore. The passengers too: he could see the cutter, looking almost festive with the many coloured dresses and parasols of the ladies and the jackets and fancy waistcoats of the men. Abercrombie was there, sitting aloof in the stern sheets, hoping no doubt to beat the other captains to the governor. There was no sign of Susan.

Then he saw her. The cutter had already cast off when, on a hail from the entry port, the crew back-paddled and the coxswain, leaning from the thwarts, made fast.

She was wearing a dress of blue organdie, the same

8

dress, he was sure, which she had worn on their honeymoon. Was she hoping that seeing this reminder of the happy, not too distant past, he would relent?

She was squired by a man he knew well, and despised, Sir Ralph Pettigrew, until lately a member of council at Fort William and a notorious womanizer. He saw with pleasure how she spurned his hand as she descended the ladder.

'Permission to go ashore, sir?'

'What?' He made no pretence of hiding his irritation now as Padstow's barrel chest and round, red face appeared above the companion. 'All right.' He waved his hand as though to a mischievous schoolboy. 'And don't get into any trouble.'

'Me, sir!' Padstow's look of astonishment changed quickly when he saw the commodore's expression. 'Aye, aye, sir.'

With a third of the crew ashore and all but two of the officers and the watch below washing, shaving, polishing shoes and darning shirts and stockings in readiness for the afternoon, it was quiet on deck and Kelso found his irritation increasing as, despite a conscious effort, his thoughts kept turning to Susan and the insufferable Pettigrew. He pictured her, looking as lovely as he remembered, her complexion clear, despite five years in this pestilential climate, her eyes, which were her best feature, steady, and her aristocratic profile marred only by a certain arrogant thinness of the lips.

With only a faint breeze to stir the air it was uncomfortably hot on deck. As the sun climbed the pure blue of heaven the heat haze which had developed early over the town increased, so that it was only possible to look shorewards with shielded eyes and then for a few seconds at a time, while to turn towards the horizon where every ripple and undulation threw up a cruel reflection was to be

9

temporarily blinded. It was barely noon when he went below and shouted for his steward, 'Padstow!' and was already cursing himself for his forgetfulness when Smithson, the wardroom steward, came shuffling aft.

'Beg pardon, sir, but Padstow's ashore – with your permission, sir, or so he said.'

'Yes, yes, I forgot. What have you got for dinner?'

'Well, sir, we're running short of fresh meat, unless you'd like me to kill one of the hens.'

'No. I'm not hungry. Bring whatever you've got.'

He ate as a duty rather than from enjoyment and afterwards, when he lay on his cot, he found it impossible to rest.

Where was Susan now? he wondered. Had she lunched with the governor or with one of her many friends in Madras, or, still squired by the unspeakable Pettigrew, was she delving into the native quarter, noting the hundred and one ways of making a fortune which lay open to any white man (or woman) with the necessary business acumen and determination? He believed that she was genuinely heartbroken to be leaving India.

'Beg pardon, sir!'

He roused himself from his thoughts as young Anstruther, midshipman of the watch, knocked at the open door.

'Yes?'

'Mr Aitken's compliments, sir, and there's a boat pulling out from shore.'

'Well?'

'It's a launch, sir, flying a pennant. Mr Aitken thinks it may be the governor.'

'Very well, I'll be up directly.'

He could not help a feeling of guilt as he stood at the entry port waiting to greet Governor Pigot. They were old friends, since the time of Robert Clive and Plassey, and he knew that he had been ungracious, to say the least, not to have paid his respects. He stood to attention and saluted as the pipes trilled and the governor came aboard.

'Kelso? So you're not ill?'

'I'm very well, sir, as you see. Welcome aboard.'

They went below to his cabin, which with the sun streaming through open ports was now at oven heat. Without even sitting down they returned to the maindeck where, under an awning rigged up by one of the bo'sun's mates, they sat like old friends, drinking Madeira and shifting their chairs when necessary to escape the sun and talking of old times, only a few years past but seeming a long time ago, when the French were strong in Pondicherry and Chandernagore, the Dutch schemed against us in Chinsurah and the Mahrattan pirates under Tulagee Angria were threatening Bombay.

'It's an empire we have now,' Pigot said, 'and all won by a handful of British and a few sepoys – and the Marine,' he added, quickly, 'for we'd have done little without command of the sea.'

'Or without the genius of Robert Clive,' Kelso said. 'I hope they'll remember that in London.'

'They will. He's probably arrived in Leadenhall Street by now. I'll be surprised if the court of directors, perhaps the King himself, don't load him with honours.'

'He'll deserve every one,' Kelso replied.

Pigot nodded and looked curiously at his companion. 'And you? Don't you feel the urge to go home and hear the huzzahs of the crowd?'

Kelso shook his head. 'I'll never leave India, not while there's work to be done. We have an empire, it's true, but it still has to be defended.'

'I'm sure you're right, only here in the Carnatic, with the French leaving Pondicherry and the nawab well disposed it's sometimes difficult to remember what it was like a few years back.'

'You're safe,' Kelso agreed, 'at least for the moment, but Vansittart in Fort William still has his problems. With the French and the Dutch acknowledging defeat our star is in the ascendent, but Bengal is too rich a prize to be lightly conceded.'

Pigot nodded. 'I hear that Mir Jaffir, whom Clive appointed, is proving a difficult ally.'

'He'll betray us as soon as he feels strong enough. He's tried it once already.'

Pigot held up his glass so that the light, reflecting through the Madeira, cast a pattern on the deck. 'And Malabar? How do you rate our prospects there?'

'As sound as they've ever been, I would have thought, although you're probably a better judge of that.'

Pigot drank and then set his glass on the deck. 'I had some disturbing information, information which might affect our position there. That's why I had to see you.'

'About the Mahrattans?'

'Indirectly.' Pigot looked at him in mild surprise. 'How did you know?'

'When you have a prosperous settlement like Bombay, surrounded by millions – literally millions – of warlike and hostile tribesmen you know where to look for trouble.'

'Yes. I was forgetting. You've had your skirmishes with the Mahrattans before.'

'Several times. It's only three, four years since we attacked and destroyed Tulagee Angria's fleet at Gheriah.'

'But not Gheriah itself. There's still the enclosed harbour.'

'Of course. And Angria's successors haven't been slow in rebuilding the fort and launching a fleet of grabs and gallivats, which can still pose a threat. It's fortunate that our Marine strength in Bombay is enough to discourage any ambitious ideas.'

'Suppose the Mahrattans were strengthened by two French ships of war?'

Kelso put down his glass and sat forward in his chair. 'Then I'd say the position was serious indeed. Is that what you've come to tell me?'

'The frigate *Seahawk* sailed in last week with dispatches,' the governor said. 'As she beat her way south from Bombay she spotted two ships on the horizon. Hull up they were, and since Tulliver, her captain, didn't have time or the resources for heroics he kept his distance while staying close enough to see what they were up to.

'They were two ships of war which had left Pondicherry only a week earlier. Naturally we thought they were returning to France, but here they were coming in from the south-west and making for Malabar.'

'Did Tulliver follow?'

'Yes, as closely as he dared. When he was safely to windward he was able to close to within half a mile and to identify them as *Rouen*, a thirty-six gun frigate, and the three-decker *Normandie*.'

'A ship of the line and a frigate, enough to alter the whole balance of power off Malabar!'

'That's what I thought. That's why I had to see you.'

'Did he continue to follow?'

'To within a mile of the coast. He was puzzled at first since if they intended to prowl off Bombay they were too far south and apparently not altering course. It was only when the headland and the re-built fort of Gheriah came in sight that he realized where they were heading.'

Kelso looked out across the sea to the shimmering coastline of palm trees and paddy fields and low green hills and wondered what it was that made him love this country. Not riches, certainly, for he had refused with almost puritanical insistence all the bribes and gifts which the Indian princes had offered; not the people, for despite their humility, borne of a thousand years of oppression, he found them weak and untrustworthy; not the climate, which killed off more than half the Europeans who settled there and sent the survivors home enfeebled wrecks. Perhaps it was the challenge presented by this huge, rich, vicious, enervating and extravagant sub-continent, a challenge which had defeated such able and far-sighted men as Dupleix and Bussy and caused the deaths of hundreds, probably thousands of writers, factors, lawyers and members of council employed by John Company. It was a challenge he could not resist.

'This is bad news,' he said. 'Richard Bouchier in Bombay must be worried.'

'Of course.'

'Vansittart in Fort William should be warned.'

'Is that necessary? The Mahrattan fleet won't threaten him in Bengal.'

'But if Vansittart plays his cards right Bengal might help us in Bombay.'

Pigot picked up his glass again and refilled it from the decanter. 'I don't follow.'

'You know the Mahrattans as well as anyone,' Kelso said. 'They are marauders rather than colonizers, they contribute nothing to the territories they conquer. A few years back, as you know, they threatened Calcutta, which still has its Mahratta Ditch. Then they turned south, and most of central India is in their hands. Because they are marauders they must always be looking for fresh conquests, and Bouchier's position in Bombay and yours here in the Carnatic, would be less secure if it were not for the balancing power in the north which makes Chandra Nath, the Mahrattan peshwa, think twice before committing himself against the British.'

Pigot nodded. 'Thank God for the Afghans!'

'Yes. They are as strong and blood-thirsty as the Mahrattans, perhaps more so, and while they are poised there in the north Chandra Nath is unlikely to attack Bombay.'

'Except by sea. Surely if Chandra Nath is half as astute as one is led to believe he will dissociate himself from the pirates of Gheriah as he did in Tulagee Angria's time so that while maintaining friendly relations with us from Poona he can still give the pirates every encouragement short of actual intervention.'

'Exactly, and that's the position we must maintain. The sea threat, while serious enough, especially after what you've told me, is something we can meet. If the Mahrattans turned their land forces against us we'd be overwhelmed.'

'But how can Vansittart help?'

'By sending an envoy to Shah Abdali in Kandahar. We've had good relations with the Afghans since Plassey. They trust us, I believe, probably respect us. If they can be persuaded to move some of their tribesmen towards the frontier I don't think Chandra Nath would have any thoughts to spare for Bombay.'

Pigot smiled and looked at his friend with affection. 'You're as devious as an Indian, Kelso, I do declare, and I mean that as a compliment. Who would have thought that the young firebrand who picked quarrels with Aldercron and Perrin and any other jack-in-office who crossed his path would have turned into such a diplomat?'

'We are playing for high stakes,' Kelso said. 'No one realized that better than Robert Clive. If I have learnt how to deal with rulers like Chandra Nath it comes from studying him.'

The governor nodded as he stood up. 'Well, you chose a good master. He'll be missed in India, unless you can take his place. I imagine that's what the court of directors have in mind.'

'No one can take his place,' Kelso said, 'and that's a fact.'

It was still hot as they moved towards the entry port, and with the sun now low in the sky they had to turn their backs on the land and rest by the bulwarks as they said goodbye.

'You'll be off tomorrow?' the governor asked.

'Or the next day, as soon as we've taken on water and provisions.'

'Then lunch with us tomorrow: you can spare the time for that. Barbara would be so pleased.'

'No – thank you.' His face was expressionless and he gave a stiff little bow to soften the refusal. It did not occur to him to offer specious excuses.

'Very well.' If George Pigot was offended he was too well-mannered to show it. 'Then we'll see you, I hope, on your return from St Helena, in five, six weeks' time?'

'If I go to St Helena. From the news you've just given me I feel I should be making for Bombay.'

'Can you leave the convoy?'

'Fenton can look after it. It's time he had an independent command. The forty-four guns of *Protector* and eighteen-pounders of the Indiamen should be enough to scare off anything they are likely to meet.'

'And you'd transfer to *Agamemnon?*'

'I could be in Bombay in a few days.' Free of the convoy, he thought, free of *Cleopatra* and of the figure in white, free of temptation.

'I hear Lady Susan was ashore,' Pigot said, as though reading his thoughts.

'She didn't come to see you?'

'No. I must admit we were surprised. She's always been friendly with Barbara.'

Kelso made no comment.

'She's going back to England?'

16

'Yes.'

'For how long?'

'For good. She'll not return.'

'I'm sorry. Does that mean – ?'

'She's had five years in India,' Kelso said, 'long enough for any woman.'

'I suppose so, only she has always seemed so devoted to the country, even to Calcutta, so I've heard. She filled all the ladies down here with envy. They were never tired of talking about her exploits.'

'Exploits?'

'Her business ventures. Don't misunderstand me, Kelso: I have nothing but admiration for Susan, admiration and envy.'

When Kelso raised his eyebrows he added, 'She's rich – by her own efforts. That's more than I'll ever be.'

Kelso nodded as he shook his friend by the hand. 'Aye, she's rich, the wealthiest woman in Calcutta, as she said she'd be.' He looked across the water, shading his eyes against the sun. 'And now she's going home.'

2

He kept watch, without appearing to do so, until Susan returned to *Cleopatra*. The cutter and the longboat had each made two journeys, ferrying crew and passengers back to the Indiaman, when, with twilight already settling its burnished sheen upon the sea, the captain's gig put off and returned with Abercrombie and one of the junior officers and, in the thwarts, a very regal looking Susan. He could not imagine what had happened to Pettigrew.

'Will you be having your dinner *now*, sir?'

He turned, startled, to find Padstow watching with a bland expression, and he could not help wondering how much his steward knew.

'I'm not hungry. Did you bring me some fruit?'

'In your cabin, sir – mangoes, like we had in Calcutta, pears and grapes.'

'Grapes? Where did you get them?'

'From the governor's garden, sir. Me and the khit-mutgar came to a sort of understanding when I told him you and the governor were bosom friends, so to speak.'

Kelso shook his head and gave his steward a hard look. 'You'll come to a bad end, my lad: I've always said so. The only wonder is that you haven't done so already.'

'Aye, aye, sir,' Padstow replied, cheerfully, as he saluted and ambled below.

As darkness fell lights appeared in the houses and along the waterfront of Madras so that the town, which had lain stinking and sweating beneath a blanket of heat only an hour ago, was suddenly, in the cool of the evening, transformed to a place of mystery and romance. The ships, too, were lit up, for there was no danger of attack so near to land, and through open ports and from the decks and stern walks of the Indiamen lanterns glittered, and the sound of music and laughter carried on the still air.

Watching from the taffrail, Kelso tried to pick out Susan from the score or more women, some young, some old, some, born in India, going home for the first time, who danced and sang and flirted in their pretty dresses, their hair piled high or falling in ringlets over white shoulders and daringly exposed bosoms, their hands never still as they clapped, beckoned, admonished and skilfully signalled messages with their fans. The men, not to be outdone, bowed and smiled and, when requested, sang, while the stewards in their white jackets went round with decanters and bowls of sherbet and plates of the inevitable sweetmeats.

'They seem to be enjoying themselves, sir,' Fenton observed as he joined the commodore at the taffrail.

'So it seems.'

'Well, it's the last chance they'll get for a while. They'll settle down to routine quickly enough when we get to sea.'

'One must hope so.' Having served on an Indiaman as a young officer, Kelso knew the tensions and rivalries which sprang up among the passengers on any long voyage, and the passage from Calcutta to London might last anything up to nine months.

'Isn't that – ?' Fenton began, as he turned his glass on *Cleopatra*, and then, obviously embarrassed, stopped.

'Let me see.' As Kelso focused the glass on the brightly lit Indiaman he saw her at once, on the stern walk with an elderly man he took to be Abercrombie.

So she had the captain for escort now! That didn't

surprise him. If the King himself had been aboard she would no doubt have brought him under her spell.

And yet she didn't seem to be paying much attention to the captain, who was talking animatedly at her shoulder. Leaning on the stern rail, she was looking steadfastly towards *Protector*.

Kelso said, 'I'm going below. I hope you have a good watch.'

'Thank you, sir: Good night.'

He was still angry as he clattered down the companion, and a ship's boy, coming to trim the lamps, received a sharp rebuke as, overawed by the sudden appearance of the commodore, he dropped bowl and knife.

What malign fate had made her choose *Cleopatra* for the passage home, and what had induced him to place hers, of all the ships, next to his own? If he had changed the order of sailing, as he intended, as soon as they cleared the Hooghli how much pain and irritation he might have been spared.

And yet – he had to admit it to himself – resenting her, he was as concerned as he had ever been for her safety.

Opening his cabin door he was met by a waft of hot air, overladen with the rich, sweet smell of fruit. Baskets of mangoes were there and another containing grapes and pears. He went in and closed the door and threw his jacket on the cot, remembering as he did so the times he and Susan had lain there, with a sea breeze blowing through the port and timbers creaking overhead, as they made love.

The fruit was ripe – over-ripe – and the soft skin of a pear broke under the pressure of his fingers. He ate one and then another. Susan liked pears, he remembered. There had been a night in their house on Loll Diggy when, unable to sleep, they had lain together on the bed, talking, kissing, laughing and making love, while in between the

20

moments of passion she had relaxed and eaten three or four pears, a present from her friend, the Black Zemindar.

He had taken off his shirt and was filling a wash basin with tepid water when his attention was caught by something white in the basket of mangoes.

He went across and even as he removed the top layer of flesh red fruit he knew what he would find.

'Padstow!' He opened the door and shouted with such anger that the marine sentry on guard in the passage dropped his musket.

'Here, you! What's your name?'

'Cooney, sir.'

'Pass word for my steward. I want him in my cabin immediately!'

He went back into the cabin and shut the door, and his hand was trembling as he picked up the basket by the handle and removed it carefully to the table. There was a long and frustrating delay before he heard a knock at the door.

'Come in.'

'You wanted me, sir – urgent like, or so I heard?' Padstow said. 'Changed your mind, sir, about dinner? I brought some cheese and biscuits, just in case, and there's cold pork in the galley, although I wouldn't recommend it, and the left-overs from the steak pie. There's also burgoo, although I'd have to warm it on the stove, and I can do some coffee, although I know that you're not partial to the way I make it.' He paused, beaming, and asked, 'Or was it a glass of port?'

'Padstow! What's this?' He pointed to the envelope with the bold, well-remembered writing, eyeing it as though he had discovered a snake or a venomous spider among the fruit.

'That, sir.' Padstow removed it carefully and held it to the light. 'Why, it's a letter, sir, addressed to you.'

'Who put it there? Did you?'

'Me, sir! Why should I do that, sir, when all I had to do – ?'

'Answer me, damn you! Did you put it there?'

'No, sir.'

'Then how did it get there? Answer me that. There's the basket, just as you brought it.'

'Not quite, sir, if you'll pardon me.'

'What do you mean?'

'There was more fruit than that, sir. I remember distinctly. I had 'em fill it to the gunnels, and – '

'All right. So I've taken out some fruit. The letter was there, it must have been there, when you came aboard.'

Padstow's guileless face took on an expression of concentration, and it was a moment or two before he suggested, helpfully, 'Then I reckons it must have been put there while I was ashore.'

'Exactly!'

'Or coming back in the longboat, sir, seein' as Mr Lill, the coxswain, had me on the oars, although I told him that as steward I had to keep me 'ands fresh and clean to prepare the commodore's dinner. Couldn't keep an eye on the baskets, sir, as I'd 'ave liked, so they was left unattended as it were, in the stern sheets.'

It was possible, even probable, and although he knew Padstow too well to take anything he said at face value, he had to admit that if Susan wanted to send him a letter she could have persuaded almost any of the shore party to bring it. But would the messenger have used the devious method of concealing it in a basket of fruit? Why not hand it to Padstow or the coxswain or even to himself?

'Where did you go while you were ashore?'

'Well, sir, as I said, I went to the governor's garden and did some parleying with the khitmutgar – '

'Straight away?'

'Sir?'

'I'm asking you whether you went to the governor's house straight away. Are you telling me that you got the grapes and pears and then the mangoes and carried them round with you all day?'

'No, sir, not exactly.'

'Well, then?'

'I got the fruit later, sir, after I'd made a call. A young lady friend of mine, who thinks the world of me, or so she says, made me promise that next time I was in Madras – '

'All right. So you went to Russian Kate's. What then?'

'Well, sir, with my carnal needs satisfied, as they say, I went about me duties, such as trying out some wines to see whether they was fit for a commodore's palate, which they wasn't, and going round the bazaars to find some fruit.'

'Did you see Lady Susan?'

'Sir?'

'I'm asking you whether you saw Lady Susan.'

'Well, yes and no, sir, in a manner of speaking.'

'What the devil does that mean?'

'I saw her, sir, and a handsome figure she made, if I may be so bold. Wearing the blue dress, she was, the one she wore on your honeymoon.'

'Padstow!'

'Yes, sir, well, remembering what you told me, I saluted, sort of, so she wouldn't think there was any hard feelings, and crossed to the other side of the road.'

'And?'

'She followed, sir, which weren't my fault, although I remember thinking at the time that I'd probably get the blame.'

'And you couldn't escape?'

'No, sir, at least, I did think I was clear of her at one time: that's when I stopped to buy some fruit.'

'But she caught up with you?'

'Yes, sir, spoke to me, unexpected, as I was shoving me fingers into some mangoes. "Good morning, Padstow," she says. "Don't say you've forgotten me." "Lord bless you, my lady," I said. "I'll never forget you. I'll never forget the way you used to have me running up and down stairs at the house in Loll Diggy, or the time when you got me shifting the furniture, or that morning – it was hardly light – when you found me in the maid's bedroom."

' "So you're holding that against me?" she says. "That's why you don't want to talk." "Why, no, my lady," I says. "I've got nothing against you. . . . It's only – "

' "Well?"

' "It's the master, ma'am, the commodore. He said – "

' "Yes?"

' "Well, me lady, he said that if I was to see you I was to pass by."

' "Without talking? Without finding out how I was faring?"

' "That's what he said, my lady." '

Kelso's face was expressionless as he listened to this farrago, not because he was angry or resentful, but because he knew from experience that anything Padstow said, especially when his master's welfare or happiness was concerned, was likely to be a Padstow orientated version of the truth. In battle he was a doughty fighter and on more than one occasion had saved Kelso's life, but in domestic matters he was a romantic.

'So, what was Lady Susan's reply to that?'

'Nothing, sir, except that she seemed sort of disappointed. Didn't hold it against me though, that was plain, for she asked me what I was buying and when I told her fruit for the commodore she came and helped.'

'You mean she helped to choose the fruit?'

'More than that, sir; she actually bought it for me.

Chose the mangoes that was not too 'ard and not too soft, argued with the stall-wallah until he found some pears, all fresh and firm, what he'd left under some canvas and forgotten, and then beat him down – you remember 'ow her leddyship can argue – until he seemed almost ready to give 'em away.' Padstow smiled and shook his head. 'Remarkable lady, her leddyship.'

'So she bought the fruit and had it put into the basket?'

'Yes, sir. Then, when I'd expressed my gratitude, which I didn't think you'd mind, seeing as she'd been so helpful, I went on to O'Casey's tavern – ' He stopped and struck his head with the palm of his hand in a theatrical gesture. 'Lord bless you, sir! That letter – you don't think it could be her leddyship what put it there?'

Kelso watched him calmly. 'That will be all, Padstow. I'm going to get some sleep now. Call me at six bells.'

'Aye, aye, sir.' Padstow turned reluctantly to the door and then stopped. 'Beg pardon, sir.'

'Yes?'

'Aren't you going to open the letter?'

'Six bells, Padstow, and mind you're not late!'

When his steward had gone he put the letter on his cot so that he could see it as he stripped off his clothes and sponged away the dust and sweat of the day. Still naked, he sat on a chair with his knees under the table and watched it from a safe distance of two or three feet. It was from Susan, there could be no doubt of that. He recognized the paper, the writing, even her faint but alluring scent.

For twenty minutes, timing himself against his watch, he sat there, tempted but unyielding: the letter remained unopened.

Then, with a sigh that was a mixture of self-praise and regret, he picked it up, screwed it in his hand and threw it through the open port.

3

The sea and the sky enclosed them, to starboard and larboard, fore and aft and overhead, meeting in the faintly discernible line of the horizon. Sometimes, when sailing alone, he thought of them as a cocoon, a sheath of blue enclosing the ship in a world of its own, a lonely place of wind and wave, shared only by the gulls and gannets and flying fish. Even now, with five Indiamen to larboard crashing untidily through the waves and, to starboard, *Agamemnon* threshing along with bows dipping and rising like a cork in a stream he was aware of the loneliness and the peace.

Susan had understood this, even though she could not accept it. 'The sea is your mistress,' she had told him in that last, shattering quarrel in Calcutta, and she had been right: he knew this and acknowledged it, while condemning her for her ruthlessness and ambition.

It would soon be time to change course. Looking up, with the wind on his cheek, he saw the sails bellying, with an occasional ripple in the topgallant clew as the helmsman held her to the wind. A stiffish breeze was blowing from the south-west, too strong to risk tacking, and he gave the order reluctantly. 'Wear ship, Mr Fenton, if you please.'

All day and every day since they cleared Comorin they had been plagued by adverse winds, and instead of reaching longitude seventy-five as he had hoped, they were still wallowing a hundred miles off Malabar. Unless the wind changed it would be a long and tedious passage.

'Brace round the mizzen yards!'

As *Protector* turned before the wind he looked, almost against his will, to *Cleopatra*, and saw the lonely figure bent like a question mark as she steadied herself against the rail, and wondered how much longer she would be there to torment him.

'Slow progress, sir,' Fenton commented, as soon as he had satisfied himself that all the ships of the convoy were on the new tack.

'Too slow for my liking, for I'm anxious to return to Bombay.'

'You could leave now, sir. We're a hundred miles from the coast and well clear of Comorin.'

'No. I'll see you to the Maldives. You could still run into Mahrattan pirates.'

Fenton shook his head doubtfully. 'We're a long way from Gheriah, sir.'

'But still near enough to meet a Mahrattan patrol.' When Fenton did not reply Kelso added, 'They've never been afraid of hunting the deep seas. You know how many times we've come across them as far west as the Laccadives and beyond.'

'Yes, sir, but – '

'Now that they've been joined by two French ships of war they'll be even more bold. They'll be anxious to try their strength.'

'We've a fair show of strength ourselves, sir, even without *Agamemnon*.'

Kelso nodded and smiled. He hated to disappoint Fenton, who, understandably, was itching to get the feel of his own command, but he had the safety of the convoy to consider – and especially the safety of one person, one lonely figure on one ship. Was it really as simple as that?

'Sail ho! Sail on the starboard bow!'

The cry from masthead brought him sharply from his thoughts. Through his glass he followed the line of the horizon and saw, just astern of *Agamemnon*, but fifteen to twenty miles distant, a smudge which could have been the topgallants of a sailing vessel.

Cupping his hands, he shouted, 'Masthead! What do you make of her?'

'Can't' rightly say, sir, since she's hull down, but I'd take her for a fighting ship, possibly a frigate.'

'How is she heading?'

'Towards us, sir, course sou'-sou'-east.'

'Very well. Let me know when she's hull up.'

A fighting ship! He knew, because he shared, the sudden quickening of pulse that came with the announcement. Men who had grown weary beyond words of tacking and wearing ship day after day under a merciless sun would be as excited as the commodore at the possibility of action. Yet on reflection he, and they, would realize that if there was only one ship the possibility of action was small, for, as Fenton had said, the convoy with its escort could show a formidable display of strength; but that did not detract from the anticipation. Hull down, masthead had said: who knew what else might lie over the horizon?

'Run up a signal, Mr Stredwick,' Fenton ordered. 'Unidentified vessel to starboard.' It was unlikely that look-outs on the other ships would have missed it, but it was possible. In any event it was the duty of the flagship to keep the other ships of the convoy informed.

'She's hull up now, sir,' came the cry from aloft. 'She's a frigate, sir, looks like one of ours. Could be *Seahawk* out of Bombay.'

A country-built frigate, one of the latest ships to come from the new Bombay yard, she was the newest addition to the expanding but still inadequate strength of the East India Company Marine.

'Is she alone?' Kelso shouted.

'It seems so, sir. There's nothing else to the horizon.'

Kelso could see her now, although from deck level she was no more than an oblong of canvas against the horizon. He was tempted to climb to the maintop, an exercise any midshipman would have undertaken with pleasure, but he hated heights and knew that to take the lubber's hole instead of the more adventurous futtock shrouds would brand him in the eyes of the crew as middle-aged. Perhaps at thirty, with fifteen years, service completed and more battles and skirmishes behind him than he could remember, he was that already. Susan, who was one year older, had always told him that he was young – 'ingenuous' had been her expression. His idealism, his sense of justice and his passion for truth were, she said, the signs of immaturity.

'What's she doing on that course, sir?' Fenton asked, as he joined the commodore at the weather rail.

'I don't know. If she's on patrol she's a long way south.'

'And heading further south all the time. Do you think she could be looking for us?'

'We shall soon know.'

In fact it was an hour before *Seahawk* – for so on closer inspection she proved to be – could be clearly seen with the naked eye and another hour still before she hove-to within hailing distance. They saw the captain coming to the larboard rail with a speaking trumpet, and they heard his voice, sounding high-pitched, almost feminine, across a cable's length of water.

'Commodore Kelso, sir?'

'Yes.' Kelso raised his arm.

'Tulliver, sir, of *Seahawk*. Permission to come aboard?'

'Granted, captain. We'll be glad to hear your news.'

They watched as the captain's gig was lowered away, and they saw Tulliver, a newcomer to India whom they had not met, climbing carefully down the ladder. He hesitated for a moment or two before venturing a foot on the gunwale and then committing himself to the gig. 'A fancy gent, afraid of getting his feet wet!' Kelso heard the comments from the watch on deck, and continued to observe as Tulliver, sitting straight-backed in the stern sheets, hands clasped in his lap, was rowed across the narrow stretch of water.

'Welcome aboard!' he said, as Tulliver came up through the entry port, saluted and, with a peculiarly feminine gesture, put a kerchief to his lips.

'Your pardon, sir,' Tulliver said, 'but I am a poor sailor – in small boats,' he added quickly.

'You have my sympathy, captain,' Kelso replied. 'Come, I'll take you to my cabin.'

'Thank you, sir – and if I could have a glass of water.'

'Of course, unless you'd prefer rum or a glass of wine.'

'Thank you, no, sir.' Walking beside the commodore, two steps to Kelso's one, he added, 'My religious convictions, sir, preclude the use of alcohol. I hope you'll understand.'

'I respect any man's convictions, truly held,' Kelso replied, 'although I must say that for a non-drinker you chose a strange profession.'

'My father was a sailor, sir.'

Fenton, who had the watch, met them on the quarterdeck, and Kelso could not help smiling at the expression on his face. Although his attitude was outwardly correct and his manner polite it was plain that, inwardly, he was asking himself what the Marine was coming to.

'I'd like Captain Fenton to hear your news,' Kelso said, 'unless you have any objection.'

'No, indeed, sir.' Tulliver blushed. 'I'm sure that Captain Fenton will find it interesting.'

'Very well.' Kelso nodded to Fenton. 'Come below, Mr Fenton. Armitage can take over the watch.'

Inside his cabin, an area bulkheaded off from the round-house and more than three quarters full with his cot, sea chest, two chairs, a table and one of the eighteen-pounder guns, they made themselves as comfortable as possible while Padstow, whose expression of surprise was even more marked than Fenton's, received their orders.

'Claret, sir, for Captain Fenton and yourself, and for this gentleman?'

'Water,' Kelso replied, firmly.

The captain of *Seahawk* was still ill at ease, and his complexion, which varied alarmingly from off-white to grey, was not improved by the mug of turgid water Padstow set before him.

'Thank you,' he said, faintly. 'Perhaps – '

'Would you like to visit the heads?' Kelso asked.

'If you please, sir.'

He was gone for ten minutes or more while Kelso and Fenton, not wanting to comment, remained in the confined space of the cabin, getting hotter and even more non-committal all the time.

'My apologies, sir,' Tulliver said, when he returned.

'Not at all, captain,' Kelso said, politely. 'I'm sorry you are so afflicted.'

'I had some medicine, which I found particularly efficacious, prepared for me by my physician in St James's. Unfortunately I can find no one in Bombay who seems to understand such things.'

Kelso and Fenton exchanged glances, thinking of Maloney, the Company surgeon, who, when sober, was better at amputations than prophylactics, and of the Indian doctors who sometimes achieved, or seemed to achieve, remarkable cures in their own mysterious ways, but were unlikely to know a preventive for seasickness.

'Well, captain, what of your news?'

Tulliver sat forward on the edge of his chair and, like a schoolboy reciting a lesson, began his story.

'Five, nearly six, weeks ago, sir, I was carrying dispatches to Madras and was, in fact, only two days out of Bombay, when masthead reported two ships on the horizon,'

'Which proved to be *Rouen* and *Normandie* out of Pondicherry and, as we presumed, on their way home to France,' Kelso said.

Instantly he was sorry at, although none the less irritated by, the expression on Tulliver's face. 'You know, sir!'

'We called in at Fort St George a fortnight ago,' Kelso said. 'Governor Pigot naturally warned us of the position.'

'Of course. I was forgetting.'

'It was fortunate that you saw them,' Kelso commented, 'even more fortunate in the circumstances that you decided not to engage them.'

'Engage them, sir!' Tulliver sounded shocked. 'There were two of them, sir, one of them a ship of the line.'

Again, irresistibly, Kelso and Fenton exchanged glances. 'Quite so.'

'I expect Governor Pigot told you, sir, that I followed them?'

'From a safe distance,' Fenton added, dryly. It was the first time he had joined in the conversation.

Tulliver looked at him uncertainly as though considering whether to take offence, but then, apparently thinking better of it, continued,' They sailed eastwards, sir, or rather, to be precise, east-nor'-east. I assumed they were intending to patrol off Malabar, hoping perhaps to catch one of our convoys of even a single ship such as my own before continuing their passage to France.'

'A reasonable assumption,' Kelso commented, 'although they made no attempt to engage?'

'No, sir, and that puzzled me, for they had no base on Malabar, or so I thought, and they could not long delay their homeward passage.'

'And as I understand it you followed them to the Mahrattan stronghold of Gheriah?'

'That is correct, sir. I don't know whether you know the port, sir, but there are hills enclosing a land-locked harbour, a fort, newly built, and sandbanks which make the approach extremely hazardous for anyone not acquainted with the channels.'

'An excellent description,' Kelso said.

Fenton coughed and added, in his customary flat tone, 'The commodore commanded *Paragon* under Admiral Watson and Colonel Clive when the port was taken and the old fort destroyed in the time of Tulagee Angria.'

'Then you must know the hazards as well as anyone, sir,' Tulliver said to Kelso, obviously unaware that Fenton was aghast that this newcomer from England should be so ignorant of Indian affairs.

'Well,' said Kelso. 'I'm obliged to you, captain, for giving me your version of the incident. It's plain that we shall have to redouble our vigilance off Malabar. As soon as I have seen this convoy on its way I shall set course for Bombay.'

'Yes, sir.' Tulliver looked with obvious distaste at the mug of water and then, after hesitating for a while, shut his eyes before taking a sip. Overhead the ship's bell was sounding six bells in the forenoon watch, and Armitage, who liked to make his presence known, was shouting some order to the bo'sun. Restrained by backed topsail, *Protector* was pitching to the waves.

'You can imagine my surprise, sir,' Tulliver said, as he dabbed his lips with a kerchief, 'when I saw the French ships again two days ago.'

'What?' Kelso, who was re-filling Fenton's glass with wine, straightened so quickly that he struck his head a stunning blow on the deck beam.

'I say, sir,' Tulliver said, rising at once. 'Are you all right?'

'I'm all right, damme!' Kelso replied. 'You say you saw them again?'

'Yes, sir. *Rouen* and *Normandie* together with a whole fleet of grabs and gallivats.'

Kelso forgot his head and the wine he had spilt on the deck as he considered the news. If the French ships were out already, hunting with their Mahrattan allies, no British ship in these waters would be safe.

'Where did you see them?'

'A hundred miles nor'-nor'-east of here, sir, just off Cape Comorin.'

'How were they heading?'

'Due south, sir.'

'South? So they can't be far away.'

'Unless they were clearing the cape, sir,' Fenton suggested, 'making for Coromandel.'

Kelso nodded, realizing that he had to make a quick and important decision. It was unfortunately true that French and Mahrattans sailing together, no matter how temporary or unofficial their alliance, could upset the balance of power and threaten the whole hard-won stability in the south. Worse, from the intelligence he had just received, there was no knowing where they might strike. In force, as they clearly were at the moment, they could sail with impunity, either west into the Indian Ocean or south to patrol the coast of Malabar or, having rounded Cape Comorin, north to attack English shipping off Coromandel. As commodore he had to decide which was most likely.

'At what distance did you see them?' he asked.

'Five miles, sir, possibly less. We sighted them at sunrise two days ago. As you can imagine it was something of a shock.'

34

Kelso eyed him strangely, wondering if he would have been shocked nine years ago when he first took command of *Paragon*. 'And where were you?'

'To windward, sir – fortunately. You can imagine that it wasn't long before we were away.'

'Indeed!'

'Yes, sir. Under full sail and with the wind on our beam we were soon over the horizon.'

Kelso said nothing, although he was conscious, from Fenton's hrrmph! and the sudden clearing of his throat, that his second in command was not impressed. He considered a reproach or at least a mild admonition, but then, remembering that Tulliver was new to India and to the service, decided that it might be unfair to judge him harshly.

'So you sailed south,' he said, 'until you escaped, and then – ?'

Tulliver hesitated and actually blushed. 'I continued south, sir, not wanting to risk a meeting with such a formidable force. This morning, as you know, I had the good fortune to see you.'

Kelso nodded and then, quite mildly, explained, 'You are new to the Marine, captain, and have yet to learn our ways, but it must have occurred to you that the further south you sailed the more exposed would be our shipping in the north.'

Tulliver gulped, took up the mug of water and put it down again without drinking. 'Of course, sir. I hope you don't think – I mean, I was ready to change course directly, when masthead reported your presence.'

'Very well.' Kelso decided that he had made his point and although he would need to watch Tulliver's conduct in future there were more important matters to consider at the moment. Fenton realized this too.

'If we knew why they were heading south, sir,' he said,

35

'it would be easier to make plans. If they were making for Coromandel – '

'They weren't.' Kelso said, 'At least I don't think so.' He explained to Fenton or perhaps voiced his thoughts aloud as he had grown used to doing over the years. 'It would be too great a risk, at least until they have tried out their strength. Pigot has *Thermopylae* and *Maid of Kent* as well as the bomb ketches. In any case there'd be little to gain there, although they may not know that, and the risk of running the gauntlet of our entire Malabar force on their return would be too great.'

'So, where were they heading?'

'At the best,' Kelso said, 'they were simply patrolling, hoping to find an unescorted Indiaman; if so they had probably come as far south as they intended.'

'And at worst?'

'They were looking for us.'

Fenton thought about this for a moment and then smiled. 'Well, if they find us, sir, they may discover that they've bitten off more than they can chew. As I said to you this morning we can show a fair display of strength.'

'Provided the convoy makes the most of its advantages.'

'Sir?'

'You know, Fenton, as well as I that a heavily laden Indiaman is fair game for the Mahrattans, despite its superior fire power. With a couple of grabs lashed to the hull, the gallivats, and now the French ships of war, pounding away, and hundreds of half-naked warriors swarming over the bulwarks it takes a staunch crew and a determined captain to resist.'

'The ships of this convoy will give a good account of themselves,' Fenton insisted. 'That I'll wager.'

Kelso smiled as he stood up. 'Well, I hope you won't have the opportunity to prove you're right, and in any case I should carry as much canvas as you dare.'

'Does that mean, sir – ?'

'I'm transferring to *Agamemnon*, as I intended, and shall make all speed for Bombay.'

'Sailing north, sir?' Tulliver asked. 'Won't that be dangerous?'

'Life in the Marine is always dangerous, captain,' Kelso replied, 'as you will soon discover, but don't worry. I'm leaving you with *Seahawk* to complete the escort. You will continue under Captain Fenton's command as far as the Maldives.'

4

Bombay had changed from the days – was it really only four years ago? – when he had sailed from here with Robert Clive and Watson to break the threat of Mahrattan pirates for ever. How young he had been. He remembered, as he walked the dutsy road from the harbour, touching his hat absent-mindedly in acknowledgement of the salutes of seamen, Company writers and red-coated soldiers of the Thirty-ninth Foot, that this road, now lined with shops and dwelling houses and, nearer the harbour, a few low taverns, had been jungle, the ditch running alongside to catch the monsoon rains had been filled with decaying rubbish and worse – the bodies of poor Indians as often as not – and any man with a coat to his back walked carefully, in the middle of the road with his hand on his sword.

'Commodore Kelso! Welcome back, sir.' A merchant whose face he vaguely remembered called to him from his palanquin and raised a hand in salute: two European ladies with their maid stopped as they came from Abigail Palmer's dress shop and watched him with undisguised curiosity: small boys stopped their playing and an Indian girl, she could not have been more than fourteen, pulled aside her sari to offer her thin body: beside him, for the space of three or four paces, a beggar crawled on his two stumps of legs.

'Call out the guard!' He heard the shouted order as he crossed the open square before the fort.

The parade ground, beyond the barracks and the prison, had not changed, and it was almost like coming home to see the vast dusty area where even now, an hour after dawn, soldiers were drilling, muskets were being inspected and the guns cleaned. There was even a defaulter being marched, bare backed, towards a gun carriage where, in a few minutes, he would be spread-eagled across a wheel while the corporal flexed the arm wielding the cat.

'Commodore!' A young equerry, flustered by the unexpected appearance of the great man, bowed his apologies. 'We were not expecting you so soon.'

'No matter. Is the governor in his office?' As he climbed the steps he remembered with a touch of nostalgia the old days when Robert Clive would have been there to greet him and his old friend Commodore James. Only the governor, Richard Bouchier, remained.

'I'm sorry, sir, but the governor is indisposed. He'll be along directly, especially now that he knows you are in Bombay.'

'Thank you.'

'Can I offer you some refreshment, sir, some claret, or the governor has some rather fine Madeira?'

'Thank you, no.'

The young man followed him into the reception room, still bowing and rubbing his hands, and perhaps from genuine curiosity as much as to make conversation, said, 'You caught us by surprise, sir, I must admit. When the port commander told us that *Agamemnon* had come in at dawn we could not imagine that she would be carrying the commodore.'

'It's of no consequence.'

The room, with its fine view over the harbour, was stifling, although, presumably at a signal from the equerry, the punkahs started as they entered and in a moment a servant came to open the windows.

'Are you sure there is nothing I can get you, sir?'

'Nothing, thank you.' Kelso smiled at the young man's eagerness. 'I am quite content to wait until the governor comes.'

To wait, to think: there was the rub. Although half a day and a night had passed since he left the convoy he could not forget even for a moment that he would never see Susan again. She was still there by the larboard rail as Padstow shouldered his dunnage down to the waiting gig, and it was only when he turned to follow his steward that she seemed to realize what was happening.

Then she ran forward to one of the male passengers – it happened to be Pettigrew – and from her gestures was clearly asking what the commodore was doing. Whether she received a satisfactory answer or not he would never know, for she ran back, looking distraught, and leant so precariously over the rail that he feared that she would fall.

His last sight of her had been a white dot, still discernible at a distance of half a mile and at twice that distance through his glass. He thought, or perhaps imagined, that just before she passed from sight she had raised a hand in forlorn farewell.

'Kelso, my dear fellow!'

Richard Bouchier had not changed much, although it was the best part of a year since Kelso had seen him. He came hurrying in, arms outstretched, and took Kelso's hand. 'If only I had known!'

'I hear you've been indisposed,' Kelso said. 'I trust it's not serious.'

'The gout.' Richard Bouchier grimaced as he raised his leg. 'What we all suffer from eventually.' He took Kelso's arm and led him towards the door. 'Let's go to my office.'

In fact they went to the council chamber, which proved to be the coolest room on the day, for there was to be a meeting of council members in the afternoon and the windows had been open behind their muslin shades and the punkahs working since dawn.

Entering, Kelso was assailed by a host of memories, for it had been in this room that he had fought his verbal battles as a junior captain against the prejudice and sometimes sheer stupidity of senior members of council. In retrospect he wondered how he would have fared without the support of Commodore James and Robert Clive. It was in this room, he remembered, that they had planned their assault on Gheriah.

'So Robert Clive has gone home,' the governor said. 'I must admit that I doubted whether he could be persuaded.'

Kelso smiled. 'It wasn't easy, but he had earned a rest, and Margaret was desperate to see England.'

'I'm glad he's gone, although we are going to miss his counsel – aye, and his determination. Sometimes it frightens me to think how much we have won in India.'

'Yes, it's an empire; Deccan, the Carnatic and Bengal, and all achieved by the genius of one man.'

'Backed by the skill and courage of his friends,' the governor added. 'You are being less than fair to yourself and to men like Watson and Eyre Coote if you pretend that he did it alone.'

Kelso shrugged. 'We did what we had to do, recognizing his genius.'

'And now we have to hold what we have won.'

They were interrupted by a knock on the door, and a khansama entered bearing a tray with wine and sherbet and the sweetmeats of which the Indians were so fond. Kelso took a glass of wine but refused the sweetmeats which were pursued, despite the window gauze, by a swarm of flies. Outside, on the lawn the marine band was practising.

'I can guess why you've come to Bombay,' the governor

said. 'I presume Pigot told you about the French ships of war?'

'Yes. It was disturbing news, for, with the Mahrattans, they pose a real threat.'

The governor nodded. 'We are particularly vulnerable here, as you well know, in fact I sometimes wonder whether the court of directors in London realize the dangers.'

'So long as we realize them ourselves.'

The governor looked thoughtful as he sampled his glass of port. 'But what can we do? We have *Agamemnon* and *Malabar* in port.'

'And the two bomb ketches.'

'Of course, although what use they could be in this situation I can't imagine.'

'They could be useful indeed if we have to attack Gheriah.'

'Attack – !' Bouchier spluttered over his port. 'You don't really intend – ?'

'Not at first, but it's a possibility.'

'My dear Kelso, would that be wise? I mean they are Mahrattans. At the moment Chandra Nath sits in Poona like a cat at a mouse hole, waiting to attack. All he wants is an excuse.'

'I know. We can't afford to attack Gheriah at the moment. On the other hand if the Mahrattan pirates, who of course he will disown, attack and sink our shipping we may have no option.'

The governor shook his head. 'I don't like it, Kelso. I think it would be an unacceptable risk. I suppose you realize the sort of army Chandra Nath could throw against us?'

'Yes. It would be formidable, although the odds would be no greater than Robert Clive accepted at Plassey.'

'But Clive was a soldier, Kelso, and a genius: no disrespect to you, but you're a sailor.'

42

Kelso smiled. 'I agree, and don't think for one moment that I relish the thought of a land battle against the Mahrattans, in fact I've done the best I can to avoid it.'

'What do you mean?'

'I've had a message sent to Vansittart in Calcutta asking him to persuade the Afghans to make a few warlike noises.'

Bouchier laughed aloud and beat his hand on the table. 'Good man! I've never realized you'd inherited Clive's cunning.'

'I think it's what he would have done – while taking all necessary precautions in Bombay.'

'You're probably right. So, what do you propose to do?'

'At the moment not very much except, with your permission, to acquaint members of council and Colonel Ashton with the position. In a few days, a week at the most, the position should be clearer.'

'How so?' The governor re-filled his glass and made a gesture to the decanter.

'We were escorting a convoy to St Helena,' Kelso said. 'Yesterday, when we were a hundred miles from Comorin, we sighted *Seahawk*.'

'*Seahawk*! What was she doing so far south?'

'Running from the Mahrattan fleet apparently, *Rouen* and *Normandie* and a score of grabs and gallivats.'

'The devil you say! So the danger is real.'

'It seems so, although I'd give much to know where they were heading. It's possible, of course, that they were merely patrolling although I think that's unlikely.'

'You think they had a definite mission?'

'I think they were looking for us.'

The governor shook his head as he put down his glass. 'That could be serious. I mean, the convoy is still fairly well protected, but it could be touch and go if they are attacked by both French and the Mahrattans.'

'They won't be, unless something unforeseen happens.

Sailing into the wind, *Protector* and *Seahawk*, which I left as added protection, and the five Indiamen can make as good progress as any lateen-sailed gallivat. I told Tulliver to continue his escort as far as the Maldives, then to return to Bombay. Sailing before the wind, he should be here within a few days.'

The governor nodded. 'It will be interesting – more than interesting – to hear what he reports.'

5

For the next two days Kelso turned his restless energy to the defences of Bombay. It was almost a year since he had inspected the shore installations and he was less than happy at what he found. Laxton, the port commander, was a conscientious man with a fine record as a captain, but he was too good-natured and easy going for such a vital job and, as Kelso found, not a particularly good administrator. The new shipyard, which had been opened with such ceremony eight years before, was in such a state of muddle that he wondered how ships damaged by storm or enemy action could be accommodated and, even more important, how long it took to get them back to sea. As for new ships he could not imagine how one could be built, such was the apparent confusion, although a skeleton of keel and ribs lay on the slipway and a score of native workmen were actually working, although, until he came, not with any great enthusiasm.

With Colonel Ashton of the Thirty-ninth Foot he visited the ditch and ramparts which made the defence of the island from land attack, if not easy at least feasible, although much would depend on the spirit and discipline of the red-coats and their two thousand sepoys.

At a specially convened meeting of the council he acquainted members with the position, or as much of it as he considered they should know, and warned them of the dangers ahead. In the evenings, despite any number of invitations, he retired early to bed.

It was on the morning of the third day that a sail appeared on the horizon.

He was inspecting the fort at the time, and the officer in charge, a certain Major Palliser, who had been roused from his bed by the commodore's arrival, although it was two hours after dawn, welcomed the diversion.

'What do you make of her?' Kelso asked the look-out, one of the seamen wounded in battle who were given this employment.

'A frigate, sir, one of ours, I'd guess.'

'It can't be.' Kelso spoke quietly, to himself, but the major, anxious to make amends for the shortcomings which the commodore had so forcefully enumerated, overheard.

'Could it be *Malabar*, sir, returning from patrol?'

Kelso gave him a quick, impatient look and pointed to the harbour. '*Malabar* is down there.'

The major reddened and tried again. 'Not *Malabar*, sir – a slip of the tongue. I meant *Seahawk*.'

'If she's *Seahawk*,' Kelso replied, 'there's something amiss.'

It was *Seahawk*. The look-out, proud of his knowledge and glad to be reporting to a sailor rather than to an ignorant landsman, was almost hopping with impatience as the ship approached to within ten miles before he could make positive identification. 'She's *Seahawk*, sir, I'd swear, but without headsails and under jury rig. Here, sir,' passing the glass to the commodore. 'I'd swear I'm right. Looks as though she's in trouble.'

It did indeed. Through the glass Kelso saw that she was without her bowsprit, although a spar had been lashed to her jibboom, the main topgallant yard was missing, and it seemed, even at this distance, that she was low in the water.

'Send a message to the governor,' he ordered. 'Tell him

46

that *Seahawk* is coming in – apparently in some trouble. I'm going out to meet her.'

Despite his anxiety over *Seahawk*'s unexpected arrival it was good to run down the steps which led to the quay and to see Cantwell waiting at the entry port, even better to cast off and feel the ship gliding smoothly across the still water. There was a land breeze, not enough to fill the canvas, but more than enough to give steerage way, and the sou'-wester met them like an old friend as they cleared the harbour.

'Stand by for change of course! Hands to braces!'

It was as though he was continuing where he had left off, a few days ago, with the wind ahead, the sun scorching the deck, and the crew, more from habit than from actual discomfort, quietly swearing as they pulled at sheets and braces. It would be an hour or more, sailing into the wind, and with *Seahawk* making three, possibly four knots, despite her spread of canvas, before the two ships came within hailing distance, an hour to wait and wonder.

As she came nearer he saw through his glass holes in the hull and gaps in the bulwark and what appeared to be a tear from head to luff in the main course, and he saw, too, that she was low in the water.

Was she sinking? He remembered bringing *Paragon* into port under these conditions and the terrible, nerve-racking vigil as progress slowed from four to three to two knots while the pumps clanked and the sea crept ever higher. On that occasion he had beached his beloved *Paragon* only moments before she filled with water.

'Do you think she'll make port, sir?' Cantwell asked, as he stood beside the commodore on the quarterdeck.

'It depends on how she's sailed – and on luck. She's obviously badly holed.'

'Too badly for any Mahrattan encounter, sir, do you suppose? That kind of damage comes from heavy metal.'

47

Cantwell was right. The Mahrattans alone would not inflict this sort of damage. Manoeuvring their swarm of lateen-sailed vessels they would surround the much bigger ships of the Marine, darting in and out like dogs round a bull, until two or more grabs could get close enough to lash alongside where, below the maximum depression of the guns, they could remain in comparative safety while their hordes of yelling fanatics swarmed aboard. The Mahrattans captured ships or sunk them if they were too far gone for repair: they were predators and destroyers and they seldom took prisoners.

'Full and by!' With *Seahawk* making such slow progress it was important that *Agamemnon* should be kept as close as possible to the wind.

At times it seemed that the distance between the two ships was scarcely changing, especially when the sloop had to move on to the new tack, but Kelso, who was watching the frigate with some anxiety, was reassured to see a line of foam spreading from the cutwater. He wondered how the effeminate Tulliver was facing up to the challenge.

It was almost noon before the two ships came within hailing distance and from *Agamemnon*'s deck they could see the extent of the damage.

Seahawk had clearly been in a serious battle against a ship with heavier guns than her own. Those holes in the hull had been made by thirty-two-pounders: the gaps in her bulwark were so numerous that the line of her beam showed like castle battlements: the bowsprit had gone, and there was damage to the fo'c'sle head. But the most serious damage must be below water.

'Wear ship!'

As *Agamemnon* came round before the wind and ran alongside Kelso could see the great furrows across the deck and the evidence of fires, quickly doused, and the tangle of wreckage still lying by the mainmast.

'Captain Tulliver!'

'Captain Tulliver is wounded, sir,' a voice cried. 'This is Jones, first lieutenant. I have taken over command.'

'What's your damage, Mr Jones? Do you think you can make port?'

'I'm not sure, sir. We're badly holed below the water line and still taking in water.'

'Hold her as she is. I'm coming over.'

'Lower away the gig!' Cantwell cried, without waiting for the order, and Kelso was glad to note that he was a young man of decision. 'Do you want any crew, sir?'

'Not at the moment. I'll take Padstow and another oarsman and your most efficient bo'sun's mate.'

'Crocker, sir. You'll find him dependable.'

They were rowed from *Agamemnon*, now a ship's length ahead, across the narrow strip of water to the wallowing frigate and fastened without difficulty to the mainchains. The sea, Kelso noted, was almost to the tumblehome.

'Welcome aboard, sir!' cried Jones, an elderly lieutenant whom Kelso remembered from his earlier days in Bombay. His tired and worried expression cleared a little as he welcomed the commodore.

'Well, Mr Jones, you seem to have had some trouble.'

'Yes, sir. It was two days back. We were sailing with the convoy, close-hauled – '

'Later.' Kelso held up his hand, as he quickly surveyed the damage. 'Where is Captain Tulliver?'

'In his cabin, sir, with Noakes the surgeon. I'm afraid – '
The lieutenant looked at Kelso and shook his head.

Tulliver was in a sorry state. As Kelso opened the cabin door he was met by a sharp oath from the surgeon who was kneeling beside the cot and by a stifled groan from the captain. The heat and smell in the enclosed area were indescribable, and Kelso could feel only compassion for the man who watched him with eyes which seemed to burn in the ashen wastes of his face.

'Sir!' The lips moved but no sound emerged, and yet he seemed desperate to speak.

'Later,' Kelso said, 'when you are feeling better. Now you must rest. You are only a few miles from Bombay.'

A few miles, yet an impossible distance unless he could keep *Seahawk* afloat. He waited for the surgeon to join him in the passage.

'How is he?'

'Not good, sir, I'm afraid. I doubt that he'll make port.'

Kelso shook his head. 'We've a long haul ahead of us, I'm afraid. Do the best you can.'

As he ran up the companion to the quarterdeck he called Jones to the weather rail. 'Now,' he said, 'your report, Mr Jones, and as briefly as possible, for we haven't much time.'

'Well, sir, we were escorting the convoy, as you know, when suddenly to starboard, we saw – '

'No,' Kelso interrupted. 'I'll hear that later. What about the damage to your ship?'

'She's in bad shape, sir as you can see. We lost the bowsprit and the main topgallant yard: the main course is damaged but still holding, although for how much longer – '

'How is she below the water line?'

'There are three holes, sir, one of which has been plugged. The other two, caused by their heavier metal as we heeled for the turn are too big for plugging, in fact we are taking in water so fast that I doubt whether – '

'Have you tried fothers?'

'No, sir. In my opinion they are too big and in any case we need the canvas for the main course which will have to be bent.'

50

'You'll have no chance to bend a main course or any other sail unless you stay afloat.' Kelso crossed to the rail and called down the maindeck. 'Where's the bo'sun?'

'Dead, sir,' someone replied. 'Mr Lovegrove has taken over.'

'All right. My compliments to Mr Lovegrove and ask him to report to me at once: and send me the sailmaker.'

They came at the double, a red-faced man who, from the thrust of his chest reminded Kelso of a fighting cock, and a grizzled old man, a hunchback, who was the sailmaker.

'What's your name?'

'Tregannon, sir.'

'Very well. Now I want two fothers and I want them quickly. You'll have to use plain canvas, double sewn, the stoutest you've got, for there'll be no time for thrumming. Report to me when they're ready.'

'Aye, aye, sir.' The old man touched his forehead and then hesitated. 'Beg pardon, sir, but where will I get canvas?'

'From the sail locker. If necessary you'll have to do without a main course.'

'Aye, aye, sir, and if that aren't enough?'

'Look behind you, man,' Kelso said. 'There's a main topgallant somewhere in that wreckage.'

As the sailmaker shuffled away Kelso turned to the acting bo'sun. 'Now, Mr Lovegrove, what of your crew?'

'Twenty dead, sir, forty injured. The rest have been pumping day and night, and – '

'I know that. First, detail a working party to help the sailmaker.'

'Aye, aye, sir.'

'Then get that wreckage cleared. What's the position on the pumps?'

'Not good, sir. They're working knee deep already,

although they've come up from the orlop. They're tired too, sir!'

'That goes without saying, but they'll be tireder still if we're to save the ship.' He turned to the bo'sun's mate who had come across with him from *Agamemnon*. 'Mr Crocker, get back to your ship. My compliments to Mr Cantwell and ask him to send a working party of twenty men, the strongest he's got, and ask him to be sure to include some swimmers.'

'Aye, aye, sir.'

'And ask him, too, to have a strong rope ready. When – if – we manage the fothers he may have to take us in tow.'

Kelso turned to Jones and the other officers who were standing together on the quarterdeck, obviously relieved that he had taken over. He could imagine their feelings. After a bloody battle in which almost a third of the crew had been wounded or killed and two days of desperate pumping, few, if any, could have retained much hope of saving the ship or, indeed, their lives unless she sank slowly. It was essential to convince them that he, at least, the most senior officer aboard, had not given up hope.

'We'll get some relief soon, gentlemen,' he said, cheerfully and loudly enough to be heard by the watch on deck. 'We're in sight of land and the wind's in our favour. With luck we'll be in Bombay by nightfall.'

That raised a cheer, as he had hoped, and he heard the men responding willingly to Lovegrove's urging as they hacked and pulled at the wreckage and, before long, dragged clear the topgallant.

'Put it here, lads,' Lovegrove ordered. 'Some of you get the cringles threaded.'

'Mr Lovegrove,' the sailmaker was calling. 'I'll want all the canvas from the locker.'

'You hear that, lads? You, you and you – at the double!'

The atmosphere on deck was remarkable compared with the apathy Kelso had felt as he came on board. Men who had been on their feet for the best part of two days found new energy as they found hope. More, they recovered their humour, and it was good to hear their chaffing and laughter.

'A suggestion, Mr Jones,' Kelso said, in the lieutenant's ear. 'It might be helpful if an officer saw the men below and told them what we are doing.'

'An excellent idea, sir: I'll go myself.'

The cutter with a crew of twenty picked men was just putting off from *Agamemnon*. Kelso watched twelve oars, moving in unison, rising and falling in the sun. Clank, clank went the pumps, faster it seemed and with more purpose then before. 'Move, you bastards, move!' Lovegrove urged from the well of the maindeck, where broken spars and a tangle of ropes were being dragged clear. From somewhere below – the cockpit, he imagined, since the orlop was now under water – came the scream of a wounded man. 'Keep at it, lads!' Kelso shouted, noting the involuntary reaction.

He went to the wheel, which the quartermaster and a seaman, bare to the waist, were holding with difficulty.

'How's she answering?'

'Not well, sir,' the quartermaster replied, a gloomy man with a saturnine expression. 'She's settling fast in my opinion, and there's scarcely steerage way.'

'But she's holding,' Kelso replied, sharply – it was necessary to avoid any acceptance of defeat. 'There's help coming.'

'We'll never make it, sir,' the man insisted.

'Not if you give up,' Kelso retorted. 'Look, man, there's Bombay, with its taverns and markets and Indian girls, not ten miles distant and a Company ship ready to help. For God's sake show some spirit!'

'Aye, aye, sir,' the man replied, quite unimpressed.

Kelso shook his head as he went across to the group of officers, who had heard this exchange, apparently with amusement, and a young lieutenant said, 'With respect, sir, you'll not change Cargill. All the crew know him for what he is, a regular Job's comforter.'

'Yes, well, we could do without his gloomy predictions at the moment.' Kelso looked at the young man, who had a fresh, honest face, and asked, 'What's your name?'

'Travers, sir.'

'You're new to the service? I thought I knew all the officers of the Marine.'

'I was commissioned a month back, sir. Before that I was guinea pig on *Surat*.'

Kelso nodded, remembering his own days as a midshipman and the excitement of his first commission. 'Well, Mr Travers, I'd be obliged if you'd report to me on the position below. Find the carpenter, if he's not there already, and get his assessment of the damage.'

'Aye, aye, sir.'

As the young man scuttled away Kelso turned to the other officers and said, with a smile, 'Well, gentlemen, I'm sorry to have kept you waiting. There'll be jobs for everyone directly – we'll be busy enough in all conscience for the next few hours. Fortunately I've made your acquaintance before and I know that I can rely on you.'

He turned as the head and shoulders of the first man – it was Crocker, the bo'sun's mate – appeared in the entry port to be greeted by a few cheers and good-natured cat-calls from the crew on deck. 'It seems, gentlemen, that we are almost ready.'

He remembered how as a young man he had dived overboard himself to get the fother in position. He was too old for that now and perhaps too senior, but he knew that he would fret until the job was properly done.

'What progress, Mr Tregannon?' he called, as he came down the companion to the maindeck.

'One fother ready, sir,' Lovegrove answered, for the sailmaker.

'Not to my liking, sir,' Tregannon added, 'but she'll do.'

'Splendid!' Kelso turned to the men from *Agamemnon*, who were still coming aboard. 'Mr Crocker, I want four swimmers.'

'Aye, aye, sir. I have them ready.' He pointed to four men of strangely varying sizes – the tallest was a giant, well over six feet in height, the shortest not much more than five – but all, as they stood, stripped to the waist, splendidly muscled.

'Well, lads,' Kelso said. 'You know what to do. Mr Lovegrove, you'd better take over.'

'Aye, aye, sir.'

'What about the other men, sir?' Crocker asked.

'Detail two to help the fother party, two more to help with that wreckage. The rest can take over on the pumps.'

As the men from *Agamemnon* ran to their duties Kelso looked aft to the quarterdeck where Jones was waiting. 'Back the mainyards, Mr Jones, if you please,' he called. It was probably not necessary to heave-to, so slow was their progress, but since all their hopes lay in the fothers he was not going to take chances. He watched, apparently calm, but inwardly tense, as the four men climbed the bulwark, slid down the tumblehome and into the sea.

'Lower away!' Lovegrove was shouting, and the party on deck pushed the folded canvas over the side and lowered it by securing ropes into the sea.

There it lay, at first inert, like a huge log, but then, as the swimmers caught the corners, spreading and moving gently to the waves.

'Ready, lads?' Lovegrove called from the deck.

One man, the smallest, who was apparently the leader, waited until they were correctly stationed at peak, throat, leech and luff before raising his hand.

'Ready, and steady, and go,' shouted Lovegrove.

The men dived together, the two farthest from the ship plunging steeply, the two at leech and luff more slowly, their bodies clearly visible as they struggled to keep the canvas taut.

Kelso knew the difficulties. Unless by fortune and good judgement the canvas was exactly positioned the whole exercise would be in vain. If the securing ropes were too short the hole would be only partly covered, and it would be seconds rather than minutes before the fother was sucked by the inrush of water into the bowels of the ship. If they were too long the hole would be reduced but not sufficiently to keep out the water. A misjudgement of position fore or aft would prove equally defeating.

A full minute elapsed before three swimmers emerged like corks from a bottle and lay back, treading water, as they gasped for breath. There was no sign of the fourth.

'Where's Jackson?' shouted Crocker, who had joined the watchers on deck.

The other swimmers looked round, and one, the big man, immediately took a deep breath and dived.

He was below a long time, and Kelso was beginning to wonder what he would do if at the first attempt two men were drowned when the big man's head broke the surface.

'Well?'

'No sign of him, sir.'

'I'll try,' another swimmer called and was just throwing back his head to dive when Kelso caught a glimpse of wet, pink skin to his left.

'Belay that!' he shouted, and, as the swimmer hesitated, caught the man's naked companion who had just emerged from the main hatch and thrust him to the bulwark.

'What happened to you?' Kelso asked, reflecting the grins of the three swimmers below.

'Got too close, sir, I reckon. Fother's too short and too much aft. Afore I knew what was happening I was inside the hold, with the orlop full of water.'

'You found the hatch?'

'Aye, sir, although not before I was getting a mite short of breath. Came up by the pumping party on the lower deck.'

'Thought you was a mermaid,' one of the crew cried. 'Or a blue-nosed whale,' someone else suggested.

Kelso smiled. 'Well, you're safe. Do you feel like another go?'

'If you like, sir, only – '

'I'll go, sir,' came a voice from the entry port, and he turned to see Padstow already stripping off.

'All right.' Kelso nodded to Jackson. 'You've done your bit. Padstow can take your place.'

He had, in truth, forgotten his steward, who had learnt to swim and dive in his native Cornwall – as a smuggler, by some accounts – and was apparently without fear.

'Excuse me, sir.'

He turned to find Travers at his shoulder. 'Well?'

'May I suggest, sir – ' The young lieutenant obviously wanted to draw him away from the crew.

'Very well.' Kelso called, 'Over you go, Padstow. Mr Lovegrove, let out another two, three yards of rope and bring her the same distance forward.'

'Aye, aye, sir.'

'Well?' Kelso asked, as soon as they were out of hearing. 'What did you find?'

'It's not good, sir, I'm afraid. She's settling fast. Wilson the carpenter doubts that fothers can keep her afloat, although it's worth trying.'

'How about the pumps?'

'Still working, sir, although the crew have water to their waists.'

'Very well. Keep this to yourself.'

He managed a smile as he strode forward, and his voice was confident as he cried, 'All right, Mr Lovegrove. As soon as you're ready.'

He watched, scarcely daring to hope, as the men dived again, dragging down the canvas until it lay flush with the side. There was no way of knowing, until the swimmers returned, whether it had covered the hole.

Padstow was the first to break the surface, and as he shook the water from his hair his red, moon face split with a grin.

'Well?'

'Tight as a glove, sir.'

'Splendid.' His tone was curt, since he was afraid to show his relief, but he smiled as he called, 'Are you ready for another go?'

'If it's as easy as that one, sir,' one of the swimmers called.

He signalled to Lovegrove, who already had the second fother by the bulwark.

'Lower away!' Lovegrove called, then, to the swimmers, 'This one's bigger but not so deep – just below the surface.'

'All come the same to us,' Padstow replied, as he swam with powerful strokes towards the canvas.

'Ready, and steady, and go!'

The swimmers dived, but emerged again in a few seconds, one still holding the edge of canvas.

'What now?'

'Just below the surface, you say?' Padstow expostulated. 'Three fathoms more likely and a long spit abaft.'

'No good blaming me,' Lovegrove retorted. 'They're Mr Timpson's measurements, not mine.'

'Throw him overboard then,' Padstow suggeste cheerfully. 'Let him see for hisself.'

'That's enough!' Kelso called sharply. 'Let out more rope, Mr Lovegrove, and shift her three paces aft.' (Hurry! he thought, hurry! as he saw the sea already lapping the tumblehome.)

'Again! Ready, and steady, and go!'

This time the swimmers were below for a full minute and when they emerged, gasping, he thought they had been successful, but Padstow, who seemed to have taken over as leader, was not satisfied.

'Nearly there, sir,' he called, 'but not quite. Another go should do it.'

On his direction the canvas was pulled, dripping, from the water and moved another foot aft.

'Ready?'

This time when the swimmers emerged he saw from their faces that they had succeeded.

With the mainyards braced round *Seahawk* turned again before the wind, and although the quartermaster continued to complain that there was scarcely steerage way the carpenter reported that the fothers were holding and after half an hour's steady pumping that the level of water below decks was actually receding. They were only a few miles from shore when Kelso ordered the tow.

6

Bombay lay just ahead. With tow rope taut, sails filled and deck a-tilt as she strained to move the dead weight through the water *Agamemnon* maintained a steady two knots, leaving the open sea for the harbour.

It had been a long haul, and despite Kelso's cheerful predictions, shadows were lengthening and there would only be a half hour at most before the brief tropical twilight, enough, Kelso hoped, to run the now water-logged frigate on to the beach.

An hour ago he had been less hopeful. With both fothers holding *Seahawk* was still taking in so much sea that the pumps were fighting a losing battle. The water level, which at first had seemed to be contained and for a time had actually receded, crept up remorselessly, and he became seriously concerned for the safety, not only of the ship but of the men below. A hulk in this condition could go quickly. He remembered gruesome stories he had heard of the old *Dovicotah*, which sank within minutes with the loss of more than a hundred lives only a stone's throw from land in the Hooghli. With water now over the tumblehome and too much weight below to give steerage way he had ordered the wheel to be lashed, thus confirming the gloomy predictions of the quartermaster, and everyone below to come on deck. With the pumps abandoned she would fill more quickly but he still hoped that they could make shore.

Seahawk made a strange sight as she entered harbour,

with her decks so low that she resembled a sailing barge and her shrouds dotted with seamen. There had been no time to stop and transfer anyone to the sloop of war, but he was reasonably confident that, so close to land, few, if any, would drown.

Except possibly the captain.

Poor Tulliver, who had been grievously wounded in chest and legs, was fighting, like his ship, for survival, but Noakes gave him little chance. 'He'll die, sir, before we reach land – *if* we reach land – and it will be a blessed relief.'

'Is he in much pain?'

'Think for yourself, sir, with both legs smashed and a deck splinter through his lungs he's just praying to die.'

'Isn't there anything you can do?'

'I've given him laudanum, sir, as much as he can take, but when that wears off – ' The surgeon shook his head.

'Is there any possibility of carrying him on deck?'

'If you do, sir, he'll die: that's certain.'

Kelso considered for a moment. He liked the surgeon for all his rough ways, liked his conscientiousness and his plain speaking. Now he was to admire his courage.

'The position is, Mr Noakes,' he said, 'that the ship is in danger of sinking. She could go at any minute, literally at any minute. I've ordered everyone on deck.'

'That don't make any difference to the captain, sir. He'll stay here or he'll die.' The surgeon went back along the passage to peer through the half open door. 'He'll die anyway, as like as not, but that don't signify. While he's alive there's still a chance.'

'I'm not talking of him,' Kelso said, 'but of you. There's no reason for you to risk your life.'

Noakes stared at him in amazement. 'Me, sir! I'm the surgeon.'

'You mean, you'll stay here with him?'

'Of course, sir. What else would I do?'

Kelso nodded and smiled. 'We'll both stay, and if he's up to it I'd like to talk to your patient.'

Tulliver opened his eyes as they entered the cabin and once again seemed to mouth some words, but, defeated by the pain or the laudanum, could utter no sound.

'Don't try to talk,' Kelso said, as he sat beside the cot. 'I'll do the talking. I expect you'd like to know what's happening above?'

The eyes, watching him steadily, still seemed to carry a hint of anxiety.

'There are three holes below the water line,' Kelso said. 'One had been plugged before I came aboard. The other two are bigger, made by thirty-two-pounders I'd guess. We covered them with improvised fothers and succeeded in slowing the inflow of water.'

He waited, but although he felt that Tulliver was hearing and understanding it seemed that the effort of speech was beyond him.

'You are under tow,' he continued. '*Agamemnon* has a line out, and so far it's taken the strain. We are just entering Bombay harbour. In twenty minutes, half an hour at the most, you'll be safe.'

If he expected any expression of relief he was disappointed, for the captain's face contorted as he arched his back in the effort to speak.

'Steady!' Noakes cried, and, stepping forward, put an arm under his back. 'No need to talk.'

But Tulliver was determined. It was agonizing to watch his efforts. At last, clutching the surgeon's arm with one hand, he leant towards Kelso and whispered, 'Sorry!'

'Sorry?' Kelso said. 'There's no need to be sorry. From what I've heard from Jones and the other officers you acted bravely and with great determination. Your casualties alone and the damage to your ship prove that you were in the thick of the fighting. A country-built frigate against a French ship of the line is a long way from being an equal battle, yet from what Jones tells me you tackled *Normandie* and engaged her throughout. In the end it was she who broke the engagement.'

He was glad that he had said it and, from the expression on Tulliver's face, that he understood. He had been quite wrong about the new captain and he was ashamed that he had misjudged him. Despite his effeminacy and his apparent dislike of the sea he had fought with great courage and against enormous odds. From what he had been able to gather from Jones in the few distracted moments they had spent together it was Tulliver who had elected to engage the huge ship of the line while *Rouen* and the Mahrattan gallivats swarmed round *Protector* and the ships of the convoy; it was Tulliver who had returned to the attack again and again until *Normandie*, with foretopgallant yard shot away and mizzen trailing, was forced to retire; it was Tulliver who had continued to attack until he was wounded.

'In the next few days,' Kelso said, 'we shall take depositions from Jones and the other officers – from you, too, of course – and I don't doubt that this action will go down in Marine history. You fought bravely, captain, and the Company won't forget that in a hurry.'

The big, pain-filled eyes watched him steadily, and for a moment it seemed that Tulliver was at rest. Then the mouth opened and after two or three attempts he managed to say the word: 'Sorry!'

'Don't be sorry,' Kelso said. 'You're a hero.'

'And now I'm dying.' The words came quietly and without expression, as though he was simply stating a fact.

'Perhaps, perhaps not,' Kelso said. 'You're badly wounded – you know that – but we are coming into Bombay. Don't give up now. You've everything to live for.'

'Sorry!' Tulliver repeated the word and turned his face away on the pillow.

Kelso remained silent, hoping that he would sleep and trying to ignore the sounds from above. Through the open port he could see Colaba Point and the narrow strip of land which led to the dockyard. Although they were still in deep water and could drown easily enough if *Seahawk* chose to founder they were no more than a few cables' length from safety. 'Have those lines ready?' Jones was shouting, and someone – from the shore or perhaps from a boat that had come alongside – called, 'We'll take it when you're ready.'

He knew that he should go on deck to supervise what could be the most difficult part of the rescue, but he was restrained by compassion. 'He'll die before we reach land,' Noakes had said, and from the deathly whiteness of his cheeks he thought that the surgeon was right.

At last, seeing that Tulliver's eyes were closed, he rose carefully and whispered to the surgeon, 'I'm going on deck.'

'Commodore!' Tulliver's voice was suddenly strong and, turning on the pillow, he reached out and grasped Kelso's hand.

'Sorry! Sorry!' He spoke quite firmly now, as though he had found new strength and his brain was clear.

Then he shook his head and with a half smile looked up at Kelso and muttered, 'I never wanted to be a sailor, and that's the truth,' and with that he died.

Kelso stood up. 'I must go. I'll be back directly, as soon as we're aground.'

The surgeon nodded. 'It was a merciful release, sir. I'm sure you see that. If he'd lived he would have been only half a man.'

Kelso nodded and went out into the sunshine.

They were actually in the dockyard, with the shelving

beach no more than a stone's throw away. *Agamemnon*, which had cast off, was hove-to a cable's length to starboard and was running out her anchor. Willing hands pulled at the two lines which had been thrown ashore. Slowly, inch by inch, *Seahawk* edged to safety.

There was nothing for him to do, and he was glad that Jones, whose authority he had superseded as they arranged the fothers, should have credit for this final part of the rescue.

He went back to the cabin.

'Will he be buried at sea?' the surgeon asked.

'I think not. We'll bury him with marine honours at St Mary's.' As a sailor Tulliver should find his resting place at sea, but Kelso guessed that, given the choice, he would have opted for dry land.

'When will the funeral be, sir? In this heat – '

'Tomorrow. I'll see the governor and make the arrangements.'

'Aye, aye, sir.'

Kelso stood in the doorway looking down at the now peaceful face. 'One thing,' he said, 'that puzzled me. He'd done well, fought a fine action. What cause had he to be sorry?'

The surgeon looked at him strangely. 'I don't know, sir, although I'd have thought – I mean, surely it's obvious.'

'Not to me.'

'He was sorry because of Lady Susan, at least that's they way I saw it. He was apologizing because of all the ships of the convoy *Cleopatra* was the one they captured.'

7

'It was a formidable fleet which pursued them,' Kelso said, 'a European-built frigate, thirty to forty grabs and gallivats and a French ship of the line.'

'It was a formidable fleet that was attacked,' insisted Raikes, a thin, humourless Scotsman who had been Kelso's protagonist at council meetings often enough in the past. Years and the climate had not been kind to him, but, defying ill health and failing eyesight, he continued as a member of council and contributed much from his experience and knowledge.

Emmerson, on the other hand, had declined in mind as well as body over the years and contributed little, even when he was awake. He could be relied upon, whether he understood the issue or not, to vote against Raikes. 'Kelso's right,' he said now. 'He was there and Raikes don't know what he's talking about.'

Kelso exchanged glances with the governor, who sat at the head of the table, and wondered how he managed to get any sensible decisions with these two as advisers. It was unfortunate that the other two members of council, Carew and Forster, were both absent.

It was nearly midnight. *Seahawk* had been beached, the wounded who had not died from being moved from orlop to cockpit and then to the maindeck had been brought ashore, the Company shipwright had made his inspection. The governor, who had cancelled a dinner party when it became apparent that the two ships could not reach harbour before evening, had been less willing to expect a similar sacrifice from his members. 'A council meeting, Kelso, at this hour; it's unheard of! Can't it wait until morning?'

'It cannot. There is work to be done, decisions to be made.'

The governor had shrugged, knowing that Kelso would make his own decisions, as like as not, but would be in a stronger position if he was backed by members of council. He had received more than one reprimand from London in the past, but since the court of directors in Leadenhall Street were always working on information which was at least three months old and the reprimand would take as long again to reach him he was not unduly disturbed. Nevertheless it seemed strange that he could not wait a few hours to summon council. The governor was not then aware that Susan Kelso was in the hands of the Mahrattans.

He knew it now, as they sat uncomfortably, breathing the stale air of the council chamber. The punkahs were working and the windows open despite the hordes of insects which beat at the gauze, but it would be another hour before the air cooled, and then only marginally. The shadows, which moved as the candle flickered, exaggerated the movement of air.

'It was a strange affair,' Kelso said, 'from the accounts I gathered. I agree with Raikes: the Mahrattan fleet was strong, but so was our convoy. It's hard to understand what happened.'

'You mean we've lost a ship – two ships, for *Seahawk* won't be putting to sea for a while – two ships we can ill afford, lost unnecessarily?' Raikes asked.

'And the crew and passengers,' the governor reminded, gently, 'the dead and wounded and the prisoners.'

'Of course,' Raikes agreed, testily, 'but that don't

signify, not as far as London's concerned. All they think about is profit.' He stopped, warned by the governor's cough, and added, quickly, 'I'm sorry, Kelso, I was forgetting for a moment that Lady Susan – '

'I can't believe they were lost unnecessarily,' Kelso said, 'although I admit that there are some things I don't understand.'

'How *Cleopatra* came to be separated from the convoy?' the governor suggested.

'That, certainly. Jones of *Seahawk* thinks she was having trouble with her steering – why, we can only surmise, for there was only a moderate sea running.'

'Deliberate damage?' said Raikes. 'Is that what you're suggesting?'

Kelso's face was expressionless as he replied, 'It's a possibility.'

'But who?' the governor asked, 'and how? As I understand it, this happened before a shot was fired.'

'According to Jones and the other officers I have questioned.'

'And Fenton? What does he say?'

'Here.' Kelso pushed the hastily written report across the table. 'Read what he says.'

Fenton, who found difficulty in expressing himself, either verbally or on paper, had been typically brief.

'Regret to report, sir, that we encountered French and Mahrattan fleet at position 7 degrees 52 north, 75 degrees 20 east at approximately eight-fifteen on the morning of 26th September. Convoy proceeded in line of battle with *Protector* to leeward. Before battle was joined *Cleopatra* veered off to starboard and I ordered *Seahawk* to follow.

'This she did, and when they were attacked by *Normandie* fought with great skill and determination. I cannot commend Captain Tulliver's conduct too highly.

'While *Seahawk* was fighting a mile to leeward, *Protector* and the rest of the convoy were beset by *Rouen* and more than thirty grabs and gallivats. The East Indiamen gave a good account of themselves, and although two were damaged – neither seriously – none was captured. Ten grabs and gallivats were sunk.

'*Rouen* withdrew early in the engagement, although as far as we could see she was undamaged, but when at last the Mahrattan fleet retreated we saw that she had joined her sister ship *Normandie* and between them, with the help of perhaps a dozen gallivats, had taken *Cleopatra*.

'I hope you will appreciate my feelings, sir, knowing that Lady Susan was aboard, but, before God, there was nothing I could do. *Seahawk* was so badly holed that she was helpless. The French ships with their captive were now some miles distant and, with the wind on their beam, were rapidly making the horizon. Even if I had deserted the convoy and set off in pursuit I would have had small hope of catching them.

'In the circumstances, I decided to follow my orders, that is, to continue with the convoy to St Helena and then return. *Seahawk* I sent to Bombay with this dispatch.

'When I return, sir, I will give a fuller account and, if necessary, answer for my conduct. In the meantime may God grant that you speedily recapture *Cleopatra* and rescue Lady Susan and the other passengers.'

'Fine sentiments!' Emmerson remarked. 'But why the devil didn't he rescue them himself?'

'Because he is a sailor,' Kelso said, 'and a good captain. It would have been unforgivable to risk four Indiamen for one.'

'*You* say that?' Emmerson asked. 'Don't you care that Lady Susan was captured?'

He was tired and ill, for it had been a long, hot day, but he came to his senses with a start when he saw Kelso's expression. 'Damn you!' Kelso said. 'You dare to say that!

It's my wife they've taken, those damned savages – don't you understand? My wife!'

Emmerson retreated at once and seemed genuinely contrite. 'My apologies, Kelso. I didn't mean – '

'She'll be all right,' the governor said, quickly, 'she and the other passengers. Don't forget that although they are in the hands of Mahrattans there are Frenchmen in command.'

'I hope you are right,' Kelso replied, 'although I think it less than certain that those savages will listen to French officers.'

'They'll listen,' the governor said, 'at least for the present, for they will be savouring their new power. Chandra Nath in Poona and Kishun Roy in Gheriah will have realized the effectiveness of their alliance.'

It was still hot, although occasionally, as the wind freshened, they would feel a cool breeze from the sea. Outside, the world was in darkness, although a lantern shone in the guardroom and the lamps which hung from the trees beside the drive were still alight. Somewhere, outside the walls, a dog was howling.

'I trust Fenton,' Kelso said, at last, 'and we'll not have the full story until he returns. I expect that there are some things he can explain which at present I don't understand, but we'd be wasting our time to speculate, and time is what we lack.'

'What happened to *Cleopatra*'s steering, for instance?' Raikes suggested.

'And what delayed the convoy after I left. Even beating to windward they should have been farther west, and, in any event, given a start, they should not have been caught by lateen-sailed gallivats.'

The governor said, 'Well as you say, it would be useless to speculate. The question is, what do we do?'

'We rescue *Cleopatra*.'

They looked at Kelso guardedly, not wishing to commit themselves, but thinking, no doubt, that he could hardly be serious.

'Rescue her?' the governor asked. 'How?'

'By an assault on Gheriah if necessary.'

They protested immediately, as he had expected, and Raikes cried, 'You must be daft, man! Do you want the Mahrattan army round our ears?'

'Not if we can avoid it, but if Robert Clive were here I'm sure he would say that it's a challenge we'll have to meet sooner or later.'

'Well, he's not here, thank the Lord!' Raikes retorted. 'And you're crazy if you think that we could ever defeat a hundred thousand Mahrattans.'

'We might,' Kelso said, 'with courage.'

Raikes' thin face turned white with anger. 'Courage is it? Well, if you're implying that I'm afraid, or that I lack – '

'I'm implying nothing,' Kelso said, 'simply stating facts. Clive met odds like these at Plassey and won. We'd be wrong to assume that we might not do the same.'

The governor shook his head. 'All the same, Kelso, I don't like it. As I told you before, I consider it an unacceptable risk.'

'At the present, yes: I agree.'

'So? What do you propose? That we wait for *Protector*?'

Kelso moved impatiently. 'She'll be gone five or six weeks, probably more. If you think that I'm going to leave my wife in the hands of those savages – '

'All right.' The governor made a placatory gesture with his hands. 'What do you suggest?'

'That I take a small force south. *Agamemnon* is in port. She could be re-stocked and victualled by tomorrow noon.'

The governor's expression showed his doubts. 'With what object? What would you hope to achieve?'

71

'I'm not sure. One thing is certain, whether we attack the Mahrattans now or later someone will have to reconnoitre.'

'That makes sense,' Emmerson said, 'to reconnoitre.'

'Then again,' Kelso added, 'if conditions are right and we can approach unobserved we might try a cutting-out expedition.'

8

With the wind on her beam and a moderate sea running *Agamemnon* sailed southwards into the sun. She was following the usual course taken by Company ships on patrol or when ferrying dispatches to Madras, and, mindful of the need for secrecy, he had told Padstow to spread the rumour that they were making for Coromandel.

It was impossible to be too careful. He remembered how as a young man, fighting these same Mahrattans, he had been betrayed by the daughter of his bouwerchie, and there was scarcely a tavern or bazaar in Bombay which did not hide a Mahrattan sympathizer. The brothels, too, were notorious centres of gossip, even though the girls who frequented them, whether young Indians or hard-bitten Europeans, all swore eternal devotion to the British.

Only Cantwell knew their true destination and he, proud and delighted to be sailing with the commodore and thinking, no doubt, that his chances of promotion would not be hurt by a successful mission, was full of enthusiasm

'We could change course, sir, after dark and lie in towards land. In that way we'd avoid Mahrattan patrols.'

'Although we'd be seen by every fishing boat and villager ashore.'

Kelso could not bring himself to be hard on the young man – he had been young himself not so long ago and probably as impetuous – but he missed Fenton's taciturnity.

'Yes, sir. I only meant – '

'What we will do,' Kelso said, anxious to end this useless discussion – useless because he knew exactly what he intended, 'will be to continue south for three days as though we were making for Comorin. We'll be seen by Mahrattan patrols, you say: so much the better. As long as they believe that we are not interested in Gheriah but are making for Fort St George, possibly for reinforcements, the more chance we shall have. Surprise will be our best weapon, and we must hope that they won't even consider that we might attack a defended harbour, protected by a fort and the guns ashore, not to mention a hazardous approach and the French ships in the bay, with anything as insignificant as a sloop.'

He smiled slightly to soften the rebuke, which, he was glad to see, the young captain took in good part.

'Sail ho! Sail dead ahead!'

'Up you go, Jacklin,' Kelso said, to the midshipman of the watch. 'See what you make of her.' She could be anything, from a fishing vessel to a ship of war, and, even with the weather gage, *Agamemnon* was vulnerable.

He watched the young midshipman running, agile as a monkey, up the shrouds, out by the futtocks to the maintop where, scarcely out of breath, he took a glass from his pocket and fastened it on the horizon. 'Something small, sir,' he shouted, in a minute. 'Lateen sails, could be a gallivat.'

A Mahrattan patrol vessel no doubt.

'Watch how she reacts,' Kelso shouted. 'Report when she alters course.'

'Aye, aye, sir.'

Unless she was merely the scouting vessel for more ships over the horizon she was hardly likely to chance an encounter with a sloop of war.

'Altering course now, sir,' came the cry from maintop, 'turning before the wind.'

Running for safety, he thought, knowing that the bigger ship would not follow towards a lee shore. That was the difficulty of fighting Mahrattans: their small, lateen-sailed vessels were faster and more manoeuvrable than any Company ship, and this elusiveness tended to counterbalance their lack of fire power. When they could get to close quarters, of course, they were deadly, for they hunted in packs, usually accompanied by the even smaller grabs, and the sight, and sound, of screaming natives swarming over the bulwarks were a captain's nightmare.

'Steady as she goes!' he said to he helmsman. A Company vessel making the long voyage to Coromandel would not be diverted by a gallivat.

They continued southwards all day, and at nightfall, reducing canvas only be a reef in the mainsail, ploughed on through the darkness at a steady eight knots. Most captains would have reduced to jibs and gaff topsail, for the risk of collision in these frequented sea lanes was far from negligible, but if Cantwell feared for the safety of his ship he had too much confidence in his commodore, and perhaps too much thought for promotion, to demur.

At dawn they emerged into a world of emptiness, with sea and sky their only companions. Towards noon they sighted another patrol of two grabs and a gallivat, but if the Mahrattan commander considered a challenge he must have decided against it.

Another night, another day and towards nightfall of the third day *Agamemnon* lay off Gheriah. Through his glass Kelso saw the town and harbour, with green hills surrounding, and, beyond, the blue line of the Ghats. There was a headland, which he remembered well, protecting the harbour and, to the south, a line of sandbanks which made entry without a pilot difficult. He could even see, at a distance of ten miles, the new fort, built lower down on the headland than the one they had destroyed, and doubtless more effective since its guns would be less restricted by angles of depression. Safe at anchor and protected by fort and headland were the ships and prizes of the French-Mahrattan fleet.

'A formidable challenge, sir,' Cantwell remarked, as he stood beside the commodore with his glass.

'Yes, but one we must meet.' He spoke more to himself, voicing his thoughts, and he was vaguely annoyed when the captain answered.

'How long do you think that will be, sir? Surely we're not strong enough yet, especially with *Seahawk* out of action. Shan't we have to wait for reinforcements from Coromandel and Bengal?'

'We'll see. In the meantime we have a more immediate job.'

'To retake *Cleopatra*.' The young man smiled in anticipation. 'Well, sir, it will be a feather in our caps if we can do it.'

'I was thinking more of passengers and crew.'

Or of one passenger. Although he was as concerned as anyone about the fate of Abercrombie and his crew and those wretched hostages of fate, the passengers, he could not turn his thoughts from Susan. Knowing from experience the innate cruelty of the Mahrattans he preferred not to think what indignities she might suffer or under what conditions she, and the other passengers, were living. He could only hope that Lemarchand, the French commander, was strong enough to defend them against their allies.

'How many were captured altogether, sir?' Cantwell asked.

'Apart from the captain and crew there were forty passengers.'

'Were there many females?'

'Twenty-five, as far as we know, including six children. Two were babies in arms.'

Cantwell remained silent.

'You realize,' Kelso said, 'why this mission has to succeed.'

'Yes, sir.'

What chance was there, Kelso thought, that Lemarchand's remonstrances would be sufficient? To the Mahrattan, woman was a plaything and a drudge, to be beaten, driven to work while her master rested, or enjoyed. Was there any reason why an English woman should not be similarly treated?

'When shall we be altering course, sir?'

'Not yet. We'll wait until darkness.'

It came, as always in the tropics, suddenly and dramatically, after a brief but resplendent twilight. As frequently happened, the wind dropped but revived somewhat towards the end of the first watch, and as Kelso gave the order to wear ship there was more than enough to fill the canvas.

'Full and by!'

They were beating northwards now, a mile or two from shore, which they could see as a darker line to starboard marked by the distant mountains and the lights of the occasional village. On *Agamemnon* all was darkness, except for the shielded binnacle light, and, below decks, all lanterns in the starboard passage had been extinguished.

Standing on the quarterdeck with only the main and mizzen visible and the dark tracery of the shrouds, listening to the hiss of waves against the cutwater and watching the line of phosphorescent wake was an eerie experience. Somewhere to starboard was Gheriah, where even now Susan would be lying awake, hoping. What were her thoughts, he wondered? How confident was she that despite all their differences he would never leave her?

'Helm a-lee!' He shouted the order and involuntarily put his hand on the wheel as a dark shape loomed before them only to disappear, on a southerly course, into the darkness.

'What was that?' Cantwell asked.

'I don't know. Probably a fishing boat. Let's hope she didn't recognize us.'

It was an even chance, but one which he must accept, for there was no time to turn about. In any case, he thought, their best hope of avoiding suspicion was to continue with no sign of alarm.

'There it is, sir,' Cantwell said, pointing to starboard. 'You can see it well from this angle.' The lights of Gheriah were clearly visible, like a necklace against the dark throat of the night.

'And that's the way you'll go,' Kelso said. 'Remember, you approach on course nor'-nor'-east, in line with the fort, and two cables' length from shore you turn to starboard. In a short distance, about a hundred yards, you resume your original course, but take another starboard turn as the channel curves shorewards.

'It's probably not as difficult as it sounds, for it's normally marked by buoys, although if the Mahrattans are expecting us they may have removed them. In any event it's the cutter you'll be taking. You shouldn't have any trouble.'

'It's not getting in that's worrying me, sir,' Cantwell said, with a grin, 'so much as getting out again.'

9

They left the sloop of war together but parted as they approached the headland. The cutter, with Cantwell, Tinnesley his second lieutenant, two midshipmen and twenty volunteers from the crew, disappeared into the darkness, the muffled oars, moving in well greased rowlocks, silent, and only the faint hiss of water at the bows breaking the stillness.

It was an hour before dawn, the hour when sentries dozed, commanders, lying exhausted after a restless night, finally slept, and even the dogs were silent.

Kelso, with Padstow, Crocker, the taciturn bo'sun's mate, and two oarsmen, was in the gig, which was heading towards the shore.

They had arrived off Gheriah just before midnight and after passing the harbour entrance had made a wide sweep to larboard before coming to rest, hove-to, half a mile from shore. Here, hidden from view by the headland, they could lie in safety, or so he hoped, while he and Cantwell went about their desperate ventures.

'Breakers ahead, sir,' whispered Padstow in his ear.

He nodded, well aware from his position in the stern sheets of the dangers.

'Two points to larboard, Mr Crocker,' he said. 'There's smooth water yonder and what looks like a sandy beach.'

As they drew nearer he saw the dark shapes of huts among the trees and fishing boats drawn up along the beach. A dog barked and continued barking as the keel rode silently into the sand.

He cursed his ill-luck, or perhaps his misjudgement, for he had been here several years ago and had forgotten the village lying in the lee of the headland. If they were discovered now all would be lost. It would be impossible to silence or intimidate a whole Indian village with only four men.

Crocker, he saw, was looking to him for orders, expecting to head out again to sea, but he was not so ready to accept defeat.

'Take her into the trees,' he whispered, 'as quietly as possible, and watch out for attack.'

It was a short haul, but exhausting, for even at this hour the atmosphere was humid, the sand was soft, and at the top of the beach where thorn bushes grew beneath the trees there was an appreciable slope.

'That's it, sir,' Padstow said at last, when they had pushed the dingy into the bushes. 'If anyone finds that they're welcome, for they'll cut themselves to pieces getting it out.'

Kelso held up his hand for silence, and, as they stood listening, the dog, which had been barking itself into a frenzy while they crossed the sand, suddenly lost heart. Its barking became desultory and interspersed with whines and then stopped. Indian fishermen were coming out on to the beach.

'They've not seen us,' Crocker whispered.

Kelso nodded and pointed to the higher ground.

They were in a lemon orchard which grew on a gentle slope and was bounded on its eastern flank by a bund. As they approached Kelso had thoughts of well prepared defences, for the bund looked in the darkness like a rampart, and he was relieved when they had approached cautiously and crawled on hands and knees to the top that it enclosed nothing more sinister than paddy fields. By dawn they were a mile from shore.

Making for the eastern shoulder of the headland, which had been visible even in the dark, they had climbed through dense forest towards the summit and only stopped when they had reached the top.

Kelso saw with relief that they had a clear view. Although visibility was limited in this early light the fort stood out like a warning finger half a mile along the hill, and, below, edging the cliffs, a strip of water showed beneath a sea mist. Out there somewhere, if things had gone well, the cutter should be clearing the last of the channels.

'What now, sir?' Crocker asked.

'We'll find the path,' Kelso said. 'There's bound to be one from town to the fort. If we meet anyone on the way they'll have to be silenced.'

'Aye, aye, sir,' Padstow replied, with a grin, and patted the knife in his belt.

The path, which was scarcely more than a track, although it must have been used to transport guns and ammunition, ran along the side of the hill, so that between the trees Kelso had a view not only of Gheriah but of the wide entrance to the harbour.

The mists were low and exceptionally heavy, which boded well for Cantwell, although Kelso found it hard to believe that the Mahrattans would not have posted sentries along the shore. It was certainly strange that apparently no alarm had been given, for if the cutter had found the right channel she should be into the harbour by now. He considered, because he had to, the other possibilities, that Cantwell had already run into trouble and had been captured or killed or that the cutter had run aground.

The path, running downhill, was quickly traversed, and it was still scarcely light as they reached the outskirts of town.

They hid in the shadows of the trees as a goatherd crossed their path and again as a farmer with a hoe over his shoulder climbed to his fields. They arrived, apparently undetected, beside a row of hovels.

With the four men crouching beside him Kelso considered what they should do next. Luck had been with them so far, but there was already movement from the cottages, Indian women passing with flagons on their heads on their way to the well, a boy staggering with shoulder yokes laden with fruit and vegetables. Out in the dusty road a young girl lay with arms folded beneath her head, dead or asleep.

'Back!' Kelso pointed to an area of scrubland which lay behind the hovels and hoped that they would find enough cover there to take them towards the centre of town.

They had run, crouching, and crawled for several minutes before the languid, casual sounds of a town waking from slumber were suddenly replaced by sounds more urgent. A pistol shot broke the stillness, coming, it seemed, from the harbour, and in a moment they heard the boom of a gun.

'That's them, sir,' Padstow remarked. 'They've found *Cleopatra*.'

Or had been intercepted as they crossed the harbour. Kelso would have given much to run to the waterside to see how Cantwell and his cutting-out party were faring, but he knew that this was the diversion he needed, an opportunity to reach the centre of town.

Motioning the others to follow, he ran across the rest of the scrubland, passed another row of hovels and what looked like a warehouse, until they came to one of the main streets.

There was still fighting in the harbour. They heard more shots and violent shouting, but the guns of the fort were silent, a reassuring point, Kelso thought, since it could mean that the cutting-out party had actually reached *Cleopatra* thus preventing the gunners from firing.

He was standing at the end of a broad street down which scores of Mahrattans, men, women and children, some half naked as though newly wakened from sleep, were running. They were all making for the harbour. If they had turned they would have seen the Englishmen, now walking easily, with little attempt to find cover, and it was a soldier, emerging half dressed and confused from a brothel who saw them.

'Halt!' He stumbled as he advanced towards them, for his sandals were unfastened, and he was still struggling to draw a knife from his belt.

Padstow ran forward like a goat at a fence and butted him in the face.

The Mahrattan fell backwards, with eyes watering and blood streaming from his nose, and before he could recover Padstow had him round the neck.

Kelso drew his sword and held it at the man's chest. 'The English prisoners,' he said, in Mahratti. 'Where are they?'

Their captive opened his mouth and rolled his eyes, for he could scarcely breath, and as Padstow eased his grasp, Kelso asked again, 'Where are the prisoners?'

With the encircling arm allowing him slight movement the Mahrattan turned his head, but meeting only the hostile glances of Crocker and the two seamen, who also had knives in their hands, he capitulated. 'In Cowlapundi,' he said.

'Where's that?'

'Cowlapundi prison.' He jerked his head to the left, thereby earning another throttling warning from Padstow.

'All right,' Kelso said. 'Show us the way.'

With Padstow's knife at his back and the other seamen at his side the Mahrattan was pushed through a maze of narrow, evil-smelling streets towards the back of the town, until they came upon a number of larger buildings lining a square.

'Wait!' Kelso motioned them to silence as he looked out into the blinding sunlight. 'What's this?'

He spoke in English and had to repeat the question in Mahratti before their prisoner, assisted by a jab from Padstow's knife, answered.

'Cowlapundi, sahib,' the Mahrattan said, and, nodding, since Padstow held his arms, 'The barracks, the parade ground, over there the prison.'

'Where?' Kelso looked across and saw a long, low building with barred windows, and a narrow gate. A sentry stood there, musket in hand, and although it was obvious from his frequent glances seaward that he would have dearly loved to know what was happening in the harbour it seemed unlikely that he would leave his post. 'Is the prison in there?'

'Through a gateway, sahib; first the guardroom, then the prison.'

'Is there another entrance?'

'One only, sahib, in the southern wall.'

'And is that guarded?'

'By two sentries, sahib, day and night.'

'What does he say, sir?' Padstow asked, clearly anxious for an excuse to slit the fellow's throat.

'The prison is there, inside the barracks, with both entrances guarded.'

'Then we'll need to make a diversion, sir,' Padstow said, 'like if I was to take our friend here and talk to the sentry.'

Kelso shook his head. 'It wouldn't work. Even if you dealt with the sentry there's full guard inside.'

'Then we'll find a back entrance, sir.'

'There's only one, and that's guarded.'

'So he says!'

Kelso nodded. 'It's worth trying. We'll go back and round to the other side.'

Padstow grinned and swung the wretched Mahrattan round. 'What shall I do with this one, sir?'

'You'll have to bring him.'

'If you say so, sir, only he's a heathen, with God knows how much Christian blood on his hands. A quick turn of the knife – '

'Bring him!'

They had actually turned away from the square to retrace their steps down the narrow lane when Crocker called urgently from behind. 'Sir!'

'What is it?'

'Here, sir. I can't hardly believe – '

Kelso returned quickly to the shadows at the edge of the square. 'What?'

'Over there, sir.'

He looked across and saw, with a feeling of disbelief, two figures coming towards him. One was a Mahrattan noble, dressed in resplendent robes: the other, walking gaily beside him with a smile on her face, was Susan, his wife.

10

She was as beautiful as ever. As he watched her walking and talking, apparently on easy and even intimate terms with her Mahrattan captor, Kelso knew that whatever Padstow and Crocker and the two seamen might think he loved her still.

'Susan is irrepressible,' her friend, Margaret Clive, had told him in those early days in Bombay. 'Whatever happens, no matter how fate turns against her, she will always be the winner. Let the northern hordes overwhelm us as they threaten and she will survive. I would even wager,' she had added, with a smile, 'that within a month she would be ensconced in a palace in Delhi, advising the Great Mogul himself.'

Now she was walking, apparently free, with a man of some consequence, possibly a Mahrattan leader, and there was certainly no hint, in her laughter or in the tilt of her chin, that she bore her captors any malice.

'It's Lady Susan, sir,' Padstow whispered. 'What will we do?'

'Nothing until they reach us. In the meantime stay hidden.'

He could hardly bear to watch, so fresh were the wounds of Calcutta and her unforgivable alliance with Gobindram Mitra, the Black Zemindar. Sometimes, it seemed, as she lied and smiled, even in their love-making, that she accepted no principle but expediency. Yet she loved him, as he loved her. This he believed.

'Quiet, you bastard!' He was startled by Padstow's hoarse whisper and the sounds of a struggle, and, as he turned, their Mahrattan prisoner broke free and ran, with flailing arms, into the square.

There was no time for delay. Running, with drawn sword, Kelso followed, and the Mahrattan leader, who for a moment seemed stunned by his unexpected appearance, scarcely had time to draw his sword.

There was an untidy skirmish as Kelso, who was an effective rather than a skilful fighter, thrust and swung so angrily that the Mahrattan could only defend, and Padstow, who was as angry as his master, but for a different reason, pursued and quickly caught his captive and, without more ado, cut his throat.

More Mahrattans were running from the gateway and were met half way across the square by Crocker and the two seamen. Padstow, with bloodstained knife in hand, stood by Lady Susan.

'Have to fall back, sir,' Crocker shouted, as he grappled with a Mahrattan soldier. 'There's more coming.'

'Very well. Take Lady Susan with you. I'll follow directly.'

Despite his anger and cold determination he found it difficult to meet the thrusts of the Mahrattan, who was a skilful swordsman, and he pressed forward even more fiercely, realizing that every minute reduced their chances of escape.

Perhaps, given more time, he could have worn down and eventually beaten his opponent, although he was honest enough to admit that this was by no means certain, but thrusting forward without any thought of defence he lunged and lunged again, and, suddenly slipping, felt a numbing pain in his arm.

'Roger!'

He heard Susan's cry, and although, seeing the Mahrattan's sword point only inches from his chest, he thought that he must die, he was relieved and happy to hear her note of anguish.

On one knee, with his arm bleeding and his sword some yards away, he looked up and waited for the coup de grâce.

'Bastard!' Padstow, rushing forward, head down, knife in hand, caught the Mahrattan by surprise. He stepped back, avoiding the thrust, but in doing so gave Kelso time to rise.

'Susan!' Kelso shouted. 'My sword!'

She was already picking it up as Padstow, ignoring the impossible odds against him, made another charge.

Again the very force of his attack caught the Mahrattan by surprise. They were locked together in combat, each holding the other's striking arm, and although Padstow was head and shoulders shorter his strength was enough to force his opponent back.

But only for a few paces. Shaking himself free, the Mahrattan raised his sword, and Padstow, with only a knife and his own brute strength for protection looked near to death.

'Susan!' Kelso called again and ran towards her holding out his left hand.

Susan had the sword. She saw him coming. She seemed to take in the whole scene with cool, appraising eyes.

Then, holding the sword firmly, she stepped forward as though to hand it to her husband but instead plunged it into the Mahrattan's breast.

The Mahrattan, her erstwhile companion, sank to his knees with a look of surprise and anguish on his face. He said something in Mahratti, probably an expletive, and died.

'Come on, sir!' Crocker was shouting from the other side of the square. 'There's more coming.'

Kelso looked at Susan, and as their eyes met they smiled. 'You'd better run,' he said, 'if you're coming with us.'

They moved quickly down the back streets until they reached the main road where they had captured the Mahrattan soldier. It was almost deserted. A few old people, too weak to make the journey to the harbour, stood at their doorways, and a small boy, more interested in his game than in the English marauders, continued to play in the dust. A few soldiers from the prison were following, but without much enthusiasm, and Kelso knew that if they could reach the hill before the excitement waned on the waterfront they might still escape.

Although his mission had been a failure, for he had intended to find and release all the prisoners, he had Susan, and he felt almost ashamed of the gladness in his heart.

She was running beside him, clutching his arm every so often as she stumbled, but apparently quite unconcerned that half a dozen Mahrattans, armed with swords and daggers and at least one musket, were following.

They left the last of the hovels and started across open fields until they reached the hill of the fort.

It was hot. As they ran, the sun, which had only just cleared the mists, beat on their backs, and the air, humid already after a few hours of coolness, brought sweat to their eyes.

'Sir!' Padstow ran beside him, red-faced and breathing hard. 'Let me stay and deal with these bastards.'

'Alone?'

'Aye, sir. Don't reckon they'll give me no trouble.'

'You flatter yourself,' Kelso replied, with a grin. 'There must be half a dozen or more.'

'I can manage.' Still running, Padstow muttered, ''T'ain't right for her leddyship to be running her 'eart out this way.'

'Look to yourself, Padstow,' Susan replied, with spirit. 'I'll out-run you.'

They were now well clear of the town, and as they climbed the hill they were suddenly startled by the sound of guns ahead.

'What's that?' Susan stopped and for the first time showed concern as she looked at her husband.

'The guns of the fort,' Kelso said. 'That probably means that Cantwell's done it.'

'Re-taken *Cleopatra*?'

'Yes.' He reached out and took her hand. 'Come! There's a clear view ahead.'

Their pursuers had stopped too, and, looking back, he could see no Mahrattan reinforcements following from town. If they could keep going and shake off their immediate pursuers their chances would be good.

The path was steeper now. They were reduced to walking, at first quickly but then more slowly, with bodies bent forward to the slope of the hill and hands pressed against thighs. It was hotter still, despite the intermittent shade, and Kelso's arm was beginning to hurt.

'Here we are, sir,' Padstow cried, as they came out to an open crest.

After only a brief glance down the hill to their pursuers, who were now several hundred yards back, Kelso joined him.

The pure blue of sea and sky was marked by a solitary vessel, no bigger at this distance than a child's toy, an East Indiaman sailing under main and fore courses, although even as they watched topsails were being unfurled, and a line of foam was creaming from the cutwater. The guns of the fort fired again, much more loudly now, for they were less than half a mile away, and in a moment tiny splashes appeared in the sea.

'That's close,' Crocker said, but Padstow, contemptuous

as ever of any native endeavour, replied, 'A cable's length at least. They've as much chance of hitting her as those dagoes have of catching us.'

'Which is greater than you think, my lad,' Crocker replied, 'unless we move.'

'Mr Crocker's right,' Kelso said. 'Time to be going.' He turned and took Susan's arm. 'Are you all right?'

'Now that I've found you,' she replied, softly, and kept close beside him to the path.

They were all tired now, and Kelso, whose right arm was a burning centre of pain, felt comforted by the thought that once they crossed the shoulder of the headland their way would be downhill. But first they had to shake off their pursuers.

'How much farther, sir, before we turn off?' Crocker asked.

'As soon as we find the right place.'

He knew exactly what he wanted and was only afraid that they would have to proceed so far that they might come in sight of the fort before they found it.

'How is your arm?' Susan asked.

'Well enough.'

'If only I could help.'

'Just keep going. That's all I ask.'

He pressed forward a couple of steps as they came to a bend and, after a quick look backwards, said, 'This will do.' They were out of sight of their pursuers, and in a hundred yards the path turned again. 'Quickly! Into the bushes. Run until you're out of sight, then hide.'

They followed his instructions, encouraged by the downward slope and the thought that in a moment they could rest. They stopped and threw themselves behind a bank of earth and waited.

It seemed a long time before the first of the Mahrattans appeared. They saw his white robe and the ancient musket he was carrying. In a moment he was joined by his companions.

There were five altogether – one must have dropped out on the way – and they looked tired and dispirited and about ready to give up the chase. Was it fear of punishment if the English escaped that kept them going?

There seemed to be some altercation, and one man, coming to the edge of the bushes, pointed down the hill.

'They're coming,' breathed one of the seamen.

Kelso felt for his sword with his left hand but hoped he would not have to use it. If they were discovered now they would have to stand and fight, with all the disadvantages of the slope and loose stones, which would give an insecure foothold, and the many trees. Whatever happened, he thought, they shan't get Susan.

Then, as suddenly as it had arisen, the danger passed. The man who seemed to be urging them into the trees was overruled, their leader motioned upwards, and the Mahrattans straggled out of sight.

'And good riddance!' Padstow said, with feeling, as he stood up, but Kelso made a warning gesture with his hand.

'Wait! We'll let them get well ahead. If they stop now they'll hear us.'

They relaxed again, sitting or crouching in the shade, and several minutes had passed before Kelso gave the order to proceed. 'All downhill now, lads. As long as we don't lose our way we'll be at the boat in half an hour.'

'So long as the dagoes haven't found it first,' Padstow said. 'And when I think of them thorns – '

'Quiet!' Kelso motioned them to silence.

They all listened, hearing nothing at first, but then, as they waited, saw a movement on the path.

'Last of the bastards,' Padstow whispered. 'Thought there was one more.'

They continued to watch as the lone straggler made his way up the path. He was clearly tired, or perhaps wounded, for he stopped every so often to rest. It was only when he stopped directly above them and bent over, resting hands on knees, that they saw he was a European.

'Good God!' Kelso said. 'It's Pettigrew.'

11

He came down the hill towards them, slipping, sliding and sometimes, to his annoyance, almost falling, and when he reached the trees he stopped. There was an air of petulance about him as though so much exercise in the heat of the morning was unseemly, and certainly he presented a very different picture from the foppish gentleman Kelso remembered from the council chamber of Fort William. Yet as he turned to Kelso, after no more than a brief glance towards Susan, he carried an air of triumph.

'So, the gallant commodore risks all for love!'

'How did you get free,' Kelso asked, 'and where are the others?'

'The Mahrattans? The last I saw of them they were straggling up towards the fort.'

'Not the Mahrattans. You know very well whom I mean. Where are the crew and passengers of *Cleopatra*?'

Pettigrew raised his eyebrows. 'Where they have been since their capture, I imagine – in Cowlapundi jail.'

'But not you?'

'Or Lady Susan.' He acknowledged her presence with a slight inclination of the head.

'They lodged you separately?'

'As member of council Fort William and senior Company representative present. They thought, no doubt, that I would be a useful pawn in the game of ransom.'

Kelso nodded. It seemed reasonable, although it annoyed

him that the Mahrattans should have rated this unbearable aristocrat more highly than a seaman, than Abercrombie, for instance. 'My wife, too,' he said, looking hopefully towards Susan.

'No doubt.'

'What happened to Abercrombie? Is he with the others?'

'Abercrombie is dead.'

'I'm sorry. Was he killed in battle?'

'Yes.'

'No' Susan said, sharply. 'There was some mystery about his death. I think you should know.'

Kelso, looking quickly from one to the other, sensed a deep antagonism, and although he could hardly welcome yet another problem he was glad that Susan had seen the true colour of this ex-member of council.

'If there was a mystery,' Pettigrew said, 'which I doubt – I think he was shot by one of the French marksmen in the shrouds – we should discuss it some other time. I can't believe that the Mahrattans will continue much farther without realizing that they have been tricked.'

Kelso nodded. 'You are right. We came ashore at a village to the north of the headland,' he explained, as he continued down the hill. 'The dinghy is hidden in some bushes. We should be there in half an hour.'

'Kalewa,' Pettigrew said.

'What?'

'Kalewa: that's the name of the village where you hid the boat.'

'How the devil did you know?'

'My dear Kelso,' Pettigrew said, with such a superior smile that the commodore could not prevent a feeling of malicious pleasure when he slipped and fell. 'Devil take it!'

'Watch your step, sir,' Padstow said, as he helped him to his feet. 'Treacherous ways for those not used to 'em.'

'I'm all right, blast you!' Pettigrew said, shaking himself free, and paying the penalty by falling again almost immediately.

'Treacherous ways,' Padstow repeated, as he walked on, shaking his head.

It was some minutes before Pettigrew was composed enough to talk, and they were continuing more easily down the bed of a dried up stream before Kelso asked again, 'How did you know where we had hidden the boat?'

'My dear fellow, in my privileged position as special prisoner I have not been entirely idle. I have seen Mahrattan maps – without their knowledge, of course – and it was in this direction that I planned our escape.'

'Good! I'd like to hear your plans when we get aboard.'

Pettigrew gave him a quizzical glance. 'So you're interested in the other prisoners as well?'

'We came to rescue them all,' Kelso replied, in a level tone, 'or at least to find out where they are held. It was pure chance that Susan happened to be crossing the square.'

'With Bedi Roy, Kishun's brother.'

'So that's who he was.' He wanted to ask more but was restrained by the thought of Pettigrew's malice and perhaps from fear of what he might hear. Susan, escorted by Padstow, was following some twenty paces behind.

'Oh, yes, Lady Susan had friends in high places all right. I never doubted that she would escape.'

Kelso said nothing. Pettigrew had been with them in Calcutta, he remembered, and whether he knew the truth or even part of it he would certainly have heard rumours. That Susan had entered a man's world and by forming a business alliance with the Black Zemindar, Gobindram Mitra, and, using methods which at best could only be described as dubious, had fulfilled her promise to make herself the richest woman in Bengal was common knowledge. Rumour had it that if Kelso had not ordered his wife to England even worse scandals would have followed.

They were leaving the headland now, and the path led down a more gentle slope between a scrubland of sweet-scented bushes to the paddy fields and the sea. Women were working there, knee deep in water, but they showed no signs of alarm or even much interest, beyond stretching aching backs and watching with hands shading their eyes as the strangers passed. As they cleared the bund Kelso saw that the villagers had discovered the boat.

It was on the beach, surrounded by a crowd of men and boys who were examining it curiously and looking out to sea from time to time as though they expected another boat crew to come and claim it.

Agamemnon was out there, looking picturesque, with sails furled, as she moved gently to the swell. There was no sign of *Cleopatra*.

'You hear that, sir?' Crocker asked.

'Yes.' Kelso held up his hand so that they all heard the boom of guns from beyond the hill. If the East India-man was still free and undamaged she should soon be appearing round the headland. 'Quickly! There's no time to lose.'

The men on the beach retreated as they saw the English party emerging from the trees, and although some held machetes and one had a fishing spear they did not appear hostile. Nevertheless, Kelso watched them carefully as he crossed the sand, for, from experience, he knew that the Indian is often most dangerous when he appears docile.

'Get her into the water, Mr Crocker,' Kelso ordered, 'but handsomely. We don't want them to think we're afraid.'

The fishermen, some twenty strong, stood back, between the dinghy and the sea, and only moved, and then reluctantly, when the Englishmen pushed her towards the water.

'Out, you heathen bastards!' Padstow shouted, as with head down and half blinded with sweat he thrust a way through the silent throng. The fishermen gave way, but only sufficiently for the boat to pass. As soon as it had gone and even before it had reached the water they closed ranks.

'Come,' Kelso said to Susan. 'The sooner we get out of here the better.'

'What!' Pettigrew remarked. 'Surely the great Kelso doesn't fear a few Indians?'

'Hold your tongue!' Kelso retorted, 'and keep with us. We're not safe yet.'

They advanced down the beach, the two men flanking Susan, and approached the fishermen who watched them with blank expressions but without any sign that they intended to let them pass.

'Out of my way!' Kelso ordered, stepping forward and, when the nearest Indian did not obey, pushing him roughly aside.

His action was like the touch of linstock to the chamber. The Indians, who one moment had been quiet but sullen, were suddenly fighting mad. Slashing with machetes and with their bare hands they attacked the two men and the woman and had all but engulfed them before Padstow and his three companions came at them from the rear.

'Out, you bastards, out!'

Padstow, who loved a fight at any time, was incensed that it was his master who was being attacked, and, so fierce was his assault, that the Indians quickly lost heart. They fell back a few paces, and then, as Padstow threatened, to a safe distance of several yards.

'Are you all right?'

Kneeling beside Susan, who had fallen in the scrimmage, Kelso put his arm round her shoulder and lifted her to a sitting position.

'That was a bit sudden.' She looked up at him and smiled.

Their faces were only inches apart. He felt the warmth of her, the softness of her body and smelled the faint fragrance of her hair. Her eyes, meeting his, were full of love.

'Susan!' He was too self-conscious to kiss her, but he knew, and she knew, that their quarrel was over. Whatever she had done – and he still had to hear her explanation of her friendship with Bedi Roy – he could forgive her and, ignoring scandal, forget her misdemeanours until the next time.

'Come!' He helped her to her feet and held her arm as they approached the dinghy.

'Never trust a heathen bastard, sir,' Padstow greeted, cheerfully. 'That's what I say.'

Pettigrew, who was still brushing sand from his jacket and from his breeches, said nothing.

They sat in the dinghy, Susan and Kelso in the stern sheets and Pettigrew, to his disgust, uncomfortably in the bows. As Padstow and another seaman pushed them through the shallow water the Indians, gathering courage, looked for stones to hurl, but, so weak were their efforts, not one landed near the gig.

They were only a cable's length from *Agamemnon* when *Cleopatra* cleared the headland.

12

Agamemnon was like a well-trained fighter, stripped to the waist, with knuckles bound, impatient for action. As he came through the entry port Kelso saw that decks had been doused and sanded, water buckets placed by trunnions and at the mainmast and that guns had been run out. Along the maindeck crews were already kneeling beside carriages while the master gunners, with linstocks burning, were waiting with handspikes and mallets for the order to adjust line and elevation. The watch on deck were standing by sheets, braces and reef tackles.

'All canvas, Mr Lemmon, if you please,' Kelso said, as he ran up the companion to the quarterdeck. 'Quartermaster, bring her before the wind.'

Within minutes, as the sails were spread and sheeted home and the wind, now on the quarter, filled the canvas *Agamemnon* was transformed from a thing of beauty to an aggressive fighting ship. With decks a-tilt and a line of foam streaming from her bows she plunged towards the headland and the open sea. *Cleopatra* was just appearing.

'I imagine you'll not want us on deck?' a voice said, and, turning, he saw Pettigrew with Susan.

'No, I'm sorry.' He was ashamed that in his anxiety to get into action he had almost forgotten them. 'Susan, if you'd allow Sir Ralph to escort you to the cable tier.'

'No.' She looked at him pleadingly, but with jaw set in a manner he knew well. 'It won't be the first time I've been in action, as you well know. Let me go to the cockpit to see if I can help the surgeon.'

He would have liked to argue, but there was no time. 'Very well.' He nodded and gave a brief smile, acknowledging her courage, for although the cable tier was scarcely comfortable accommodation, with its cramped space, stifling atmosphere and noise of battle, it was preferable by far, or would have seemed so to most ladies of quality, to the grisly horrors of the cockpit.

'The cable tier for me,' Pettigrew said, with a grimace. 'I've no mind or stomach to be a butcher's assistant.'

Cleopatra with her skeleton crew was making good progress. With the wind abeam and courses set her progress, measured against the headland, was considerable, and he saw that Cantwell was taking advantage of the period of easy sailing to get out boarding nets. There was little doubt that he would need them, for already two grabs and a gallivat were in pursuit. Worse, as *Agamemnon* cleared the headland, Kelso saw a whole swarm of lateen-sailed vessels approaching the channel, while in the harbour *Normandie* and *Rouen* were making sail.

He knew, because he had lived with the problem all the way from Bombay, that, despite the success of the cutting-out party, which, at best, had been no more than a diversion, the chances of success were small. With only enough crew to man one ship adequately he had decided that the sloop of war must have preference. While she could fight there was always a chance: the Indiaman was too cumbersome to be of much use as a fighting ship, except of course with a full crew, and he decided that the only reasonable plan would be for *Agamemnon* to protect her as far as she could and to hope that by good fortune or perhaps some indecision by the Mahrattans they could both escape. It seemed a forlorn hope.

'Two points to larboard,' Kelso ordered. 'Take her as close to *Cleopatra* as you can.'

The two ships passed at less than a cable's length, and

Kelso saw as they approached that with boarding nets secured and two maindeck guns run out to starboard and larboard, Cantwell was ordering his overworked crew to set more sail. It was a nice exercise in mathematics, although more comfortably considered in the quietness of the graveyard watch than at the approach to battle. Cantwell must decide how much of the work normally completed by a full complement of two hundred and fifty could be expected of a scratch crew of forty, even when that crew were fighting for safety. Cantwell was right, he thought, in everything he had done so far, the boarding nets, the guns, the courses. If he ran up headsails, as his crew were doing now, and fore topgallants, they would have as much as they could handle.

'Well done, Mr Cantwell!' he shouted. 'You know what you have to do?'

'Yes, sir.' Cantwell's voice, carried by the wind, sounded clearly over the narrow stretch of water. 'I'll set as much sail as we can manage and head for Bombay.'

'That's right. Keep going as fast as you can. We'll follow when we're able.'

As soon as they were clear of the Indiaman's stern *Agamemnon* gybed so that she was heading straight for the two grabs and the gallivat in pursuit.

He knew exactly how to tackle the lateen-sailed grabs. *Agamemnon*, being country-built, was made of solid teak, the Mahrattan vessels were fashioned of durable but much lighter cork wood. From previous skirmishes he knew how each reacted on the other.

'Steady as she goes!'

'Aye, aye, sir.' The quartermaster, anticipating a collision, could not contain his anxiety. 'If you please, sir!'

'I know.'

The two grabs were veering away, but the gallivat, which

was at a safe distance, had already opened fire with the brass nine-pounder in her bows.

'Mr Langley!' Kelso shouted to the gunnery officer. 'Target the gallivat. Fire as you bear.'

'Aye, aye, sir.'

The sloop was only a long stone's throw from the nearest grab and on collision course.

'If you please, sir!' the quartermaster said again.

'Helm a-lee!' Kelso shouted, and actually grabbed the wheel to make sure that he was understood.

The sudden change of course brought a glancing blow from *Agamemnon*'s bows, less damaging than if she had held her head-on course but still enough to throw some of the crew on deck off balance and to turn the grab almost on her beam.

She righted herself slowly, although there was a full minute before she was back on anything like level keel, and even as *Agamemnon* gybed again they could see that she was listing

'Fire!'

The maindeck guns roared out with commendable precision, and he watched as the broadside straddled the gallivat.

'Swab out! Reload! Fire!'

The second broadside, fired at longer range, was in fact more effective than the first, for a lucky shot severed the mast near the deck and brought the lateen sail trailing in the sea.

So far, so good: with a grab and a gallivat out of action, at least temporarily, he could afford to ignore the second grab which, although dipping away, her lateen sail filled and at a speed which would soon bring her under *Cleopatra*'s stern, she would be hardly likely to tackle the Indiaman single-handed.

'Sir!'

Following the first lieutenant's direction, he looked up at the fort where puffs of smoke were still drifting along the hill.

The shot fell short, but not so short that he could ignore it, for the heavy metal of a gun battery could sink a sloop of war at one salvo. *Normandie*, the French ship of the line, had opened up too as she followed her sister ship towards the channel, although more as a warning, he felt, than from any hope of a decisive blow for she was still at extreme range.

The whole scene of battle lay before him, clearly delineated in the sunlight, and he was able to consider a plan of action as easily as if he had been watching it on a sand table at the Marine school in Bombay. To starboard and well within range lay the shore battery on the headland, ahead, twisting between the sandbanks, lay the deep water channel where even now a score of grabs and gallivats were approaching, while further back, in the harbour, *Rouen* and *Normandie* were getting under way.

His thoughts were interrupted as one of the thirty-two-pounders from the fort struck the sloop a shattering blow. A single shot, landing on the fo'c'sle head, which it demolished, scored a deep, smouldering mark across the deck before coming to rest among the unfortunate crew of one of the starboard guns.

'Fire buckets forward! Deck party! Mr Honeysett, get that wreckage cleared!'

While the dead were dragged to the mainmast and the wounded carried, screaming, below, *Agamemnon* swung across the entrance to the channel, and suddenly Kelso knew what to do.

'Prepare to jibe!'

As the sloop swung round across the wind Kelso shouted, 'Mr Langley! Target, the leading gallivat to larboard. Fire as you bear!'

'Aye, aye, sir.'

The gallivat was in a vulnerable position, beam-on and within easy range, as she followed the curve of the channel. It was a position she would hold for perhaps two or three minutes, yet he was loth to order the gunnery officer to hurry. One broadside, well laid, was worth half a dozen quickly fired.

'Take aim!' As though realizing the importance of this particular broadside Langley was going from gun to gun, checking over open sights and making his own slight adjustments with hand spike and coign. The gallivat was just beginning the turn.

'Fire!'

Any impatience he felt disappeared in a flood of relief as four shots at least struck the gallivat at or near the water line, while a fifth tore through her bulwark and across the deck. The screams of wounded men echoed across the water, and, almost at once, the lateen-sailed vessel began to sink.

'Well done, Mr Langley!' Kelso shouted. 'Now we're going to jibe, and I want you to take the following gallivat with your starboard guns after we turn.' He came forward to the rail and shouted, 'Well done, lads! Let's have another like that.'

That would put them on their mettle, for the starboard gunners would not want to be outdone by their companions.

'Main sheets and braces!'

As the mainsail was sheeted home and *Agamemnon* returned on a parallel course Kelso saw that the second gallivat was in trouble. The channel, which at no point was wide enough to allow two vessels to pass with safety, was even more hazardous at the bends. With one gallivat sunk, beam-on, and its mast protruding in mid channel like a warning marker, and the water running swiftly against the sandbank, the captain of the second gallivat was in a dilemma. Either he could take in canvas and perhaps even throw out a land anchor or he could risk trying to squeeze through the remaining channel.

He decided to take the risk.

'Fire when you're ready, Mr Langley!'

In fact there was no need to hurry, except that the guns at the fort were still firing and one shot landed uncomfortably near to Kelso on the quarterdeck. After appearing to clear the wreck, the second gallivat hit the submerged sandbank with such force that its mast snapped near the top, bringing down a tangle of rope and canvas, while her stern, swinging across the channel, became firmly joined to the wreck of her sister ship.

'Fire!'

The broadside was hardly necessary now except that it would be more difficult to clear two wreckages than one. In the meantime a bottle-neck of grabs and gallivats and the two French ships of war was building up in the channel beyond.

13

'A memorable achievement,' the governor said. 'I'm sure the court of directors in London will be delighted.'

'Except, of course, that Kelso failed in his objective – to free the prisoners.'

They looked at Pettigrew, this ex-member of council who was only there by invitation, with resentment, and fat Emmerson protested, 'Credit where credit is due, Sir Ralph. A sloop-of-war and a handful of brave men against all the forces of Kishun Roy.'

'And his allies,' Raikes added, 'those mercenary French blaggards.' It was not often that he agreed with Emmerson, but on this at least they were united. Feelings in Bombay were running high.

'Pettigrew is right,' Kelso said. 'We went to release the prisoners and we failed.'

It was hot in the council chamber even at seven o'clock in the morning, and the fans, which flapped energetically for a few minutes as the punkah wallah, woken from his torpor, responded to the high-pitched protests of the khitmutgar, seemed only to stir the stale air. Beyond the lawn, parched brown as a jackal's pelt, and the beds, which pathetically displayed a few carefully nurtured flowers, the parade ground stretched away, dusty and arid. Soldiers of the Thirty-ninth Foot were drilling there in this, the coolest part of the day, guns were being cleaned, and the military band was playing. Colonel Ashton on a white horse was inspecting the guard.

'A correction, Kelso,' the governor said. 'You went to Gheriah to reconnoitre. That was agreed. In fact, you returned, having suffered precious few casualties, with the Company ship *Cleopatra* undamaged – '

'But without her cargo,' Pettigrew pointed out.

'And with perhaps the most important of the prisoners,' the governor insisted.

'That's all very fine,' Pettigrew protested. 'But my release was largely my own doing. I would have escaped anyway; as for *Cleopatra* – '

'I was referring to Lady Susan,' the governor interrupted, icily.

'Lady Susan – oh, yes.' Pettigrew leant back in his chair, obviously enjoying the scarcely perceptible change of feeling. Comment in Bombay had been guarded whenever Susan's escape was mentioned, and although nothing had been said in his hearing, Kelso was aware, knowing the scandal-mongering propensities of eastern society, that there was speculation. How was it that the commodore's wife alone had escaped? – Pettigrew had made great play of the fact that he had rescued himself – and why had she been given special privileges by the Mahrattans? They gossiped and speculated, and, strengthened by rumours which had filtered down from Bengal, feeling against Susan grew.

'The reconnaissance was a qualified success,' Kelso agreed. 'We know where the crew and passengers are held, but not at the moment how to rescue them. That's were I hope Sir Ralph can help.'

'Or Lady Susan,' Pettigrew said. 'She is probably more aware of the Mahrattan plans than I.'

Kelso remained calm, but his voice was hard as he asked, 'What does that mean?'

'My dear Kelso, I'm only stating the obvious. I was a special prisoner, it's true. I accepted the privileges for one reason only – to plan the escape of my fellow prisoners.'

'Are you suggesting that my wife did otherwise?'

Pettigrew knew that he was on dangerous ground and that, given the opportunity, Kelso would not hesitate to call him out. His gaze faltered and he said,' Don't misunderstand me, Kelso. Unfortunately I've had no chance to speak with Lady Susan. All I'm saying is that she, with her womanly instinct, is more likely than I to have discovered some weakness in the Mahrattan defences.'

'If she has,' Kelso replied, 'she has not confided in me. But I'll make two points, gentlemen, in case there is still some misunderstanding. First, it was Susan, my wife, who killed Bedi Roy. Second, she has insisted that when we send an expedition to rescue the rest of the prisoners she be allowed to accompany it.'

'Lady Susan!' The governor made a deprecatory gesture with his hand. 'My dear Kelso, that is out of the question. Unless she stayed on the support vessel – and even then she'd be far from safe – she would be exposed to quite unacceptable dangers.' He shook his head and added, without much conviction, 'I won't allow it.'

'You'd better tell Susan that,' Kelso said, with a smile, 'and hope that she agrees.'

'The question is,' Raikes interrupted, testily, 'what are we going to do?'

'There's only one thing to do,' Kelso replied, 'as I see it. We must send another expedition as soon as possible, or, at least, as soon as *Seahawk* is ready for sea. We've seen that with luck and a certain amount of resolution we can bottle up the Mahrattan and French fleet in Gheriah. If we use that as a diversion while a force of, say, fifty marines and seamen is landed north of the headland – '

'No!' The governor struck the table with his hand. 'I won't allow it. I've said this before, Kelso, and I mean it:

I'll not risk the wrath of Chandra Nath, not even for a couple of hundred prisoners.'

They were silent, for while Kelso was the hero of the hour and had a reputation second to none, the governor's attitude made sense. No one who had served in Bombay for more than a few weeks could be unaware of the Mahrattan threat. Bombay itself, an island, cut off except by a narrow causeway from the turbulent sub-continent, was outwardly secure, with a fort, a battalion of Foot and a thousand sepoys: its dusty roads, which had once been traversed only under the threat of robbers and cut-throats, were now secure, the markets and the European stores flourished, Company servants, when they had suffered a morning's work in the intolerable heat would relax in the new East India Club: yet this façade of peace was illusory. Just beyond the causeway and for five hundred miles to north, east or south the Mahrattan empire threatened, crouched like a tiger at the kill. An open attack on Gheriah might be the incitement it needed.

'And I said before, and I say it again,' Kelso replied, 'you'll have to face Chandra Nath some time. You've been in India as long as I, you know how their minds work. To be cautious, which to them is a sign of weakness, is to invite attack. The more you lack in troops and guns the more you challenge. Robert Clive understood this and that's why he succeeded.'

'Clive was a genius,' the governor said, 'or lucky, perhaps both. We can't risk the lives of all the Europeans in Bombay.'

The temperature in the room was rising despite the punkahs, and the governor shouted angrily for a servant to put out the window shades. A horde of small insects which got in somehow despite the gauze jigged ceaselessly in the air.

110

'Some refreshment, gentlemen,' the governor suggested. 'Perhaps it will help us to concentrate.'

He waited until a khansama, under the watchful eye of the khitmutgar, brought in a tray of wine, sherbet and cold coffee. A plate of sweetmeats was placed on the table.

'Help yourselves, gentlemen,' the governor said. 'Kelso, can I offer you a glass of claret?'

'Thank you.'

'The position as I see it,' the governor continued, as he poured a glass of wine for himself, 'is that an outright attack on Gheriah at the moment would be unnecessarily provocative. Later, perhaps, we'll consider it, for we clearly can't ignore the fate of forty passengers, all of them Europeans, and more than two hundred officers and men.'

'Who are safe at the moment,' Pettigrew put in, quickly. 'Surely our first task is to discover Chandra Nath's demands.'

'Can he afford to make demands,' Raikes asked, 'when he has openly dissociated himself from the pirates?'

'Whether he makes them himself or on behalf of that scoundrel Kishun Roy don't signify,' Pettigrew replied. 'All he wants, and make no mistake about it, is to have the English out of Bombay.'

'If that's true,' Kelso said, 'and I'm inclined to think that you're right, what point can there be in negotiation? We'll have to fight sooner or later, and, in my opinion, it's a case of the sooner the better.'

They did not reply at once, and it was obvious that they were struck by the force of his argument. On the other hand – he could almost read their minds – at the moment they had peace. Chandra Nath, if not friendly, was not openly hostile, while his armies, fretting under the boredom of peace, were quiet. In a few months, a few weeks even, the position might have changed, the Afghans in the north might create a diversion, or the Mahrattans, tired of waiting for provocation, might attack in some other direction.

'Pettigrew's right,' the governor said. 'I think we'd be wise to exercise patience.'

'With twenty-five women and children in Mahrattan hands,' Kelso exclaimed, 'undergoing God knows what humiliations?'

'Twenty-four,' Pettigrew corrected, 'since Lady Susan escaped.'

'Twenty-four or four!' Kelso flared. 'What does it matter? The point is, are you prepared to leave them there?'

'I'm sorry, Kelso,' the governor said, 'and don't think I don't share your feelings, but the women passengers, according to Pettigrew, are safe. Lemarchand, the French commander, has them under his protection.'

'For how much longer? Since we've attacked Kishun Roy's stronghold, and several Mahrattans, including his own brother, have been killed do you think that he is going to respect the Frenchman's scruples much longer?'

'I don't know.' The governor shook his head. 'I honestly don't know. But on balance, Kelso, and on this I must insist, we'd be well advised to wait. For the moment at least I agree with Pettigrew. I think we should find out what Chandra Nath wants.'

Kelso looked straight ahead, scarcely conscious of the anxious glances of his colleagues, as he considered. If necessary he could overrule the governor, at least as far as the Marine vessels were concerned. On the other hand he respected Bouchier and knew that his decision was based on logic. Also, he remembered, *Seahawk* would not be ready for sea for another week, time enough to make the journey to Poona and back. If only he did not feel some personal responsibility for the prisoners, if only it had not been Susan who had escaped!

He nodded. 'Very well. Then if you gentlemen are agreeable I shall go myself. I shall start for Poona this afternoon.'

14

'Roger, take me with you.'

'To see Chandra Nath?' He smiled distractedly, not thinking that she was serious, as he watched Padstow packing his valise. 'Careful with that decanter!' It irked him that he should have to take presents to a man who was so clearly their enemy, but this was the custom of the east.

'Apart from the pleasure of your company,' he said, 'what good could you do?'

'I could talk with him, flatter him a little, in a way you, my poor Roger, would not even consider.'

'Perhaps.' He knew that she was right, for he had seen the way she could manoeuvre men to her advantage. In Calcutta where they had spent the few tempestuous months of their married life not only members of council, including the governor himself, had fallen under her spell, but Gobindram Mitra, the Black Zemindar, and – the one he tried to forget – Mohammed Khan, the dacoit leader, whose trust in the white memsahib had cost him his life. Margaret Clive had been right: Susan would always come out the winner.

'Not this time, my dear,' he said, as he took off his shirt and threw it on the bed. 'Much as I appreciate your powers of persuasion I'm afraid this is likely to be a difficult interview, and not without danger.'

She seemed to accept his decision, for, watching him undress, she asked, 'How did the meeting go?'

'Not too well. Only Emmerson and Raikes were there, and the governor, of course. Carew and Forster are still sick.'

'And Ralph Pettigrew?'

He grimaced. 'Oh, yes.'

She followed him towards the shower. 'How long before you start?'

'An hour. There's no point in riding through the heat of the afternoon.'

'An hour.' She nodded with satisfaction and, not entirely to his surprise, began to unbutton her dress.

'Susan! There's no time. I told Padstow to have the horses ready by five.'

'Time enough,' she replied, with a smile he knew full well, and in a moment joined him in the shower.

They made love hungrily, she with an abandon that would have shocked and surprised her tea-table friends, and afterwards they lay side by side on the bed. It was cool on this side of the house where the windows faced north and were shaded during the afternoon by the pale tresses of a willow tree. There was a garden below, crossed by a stream, and resembling at the moment a jungle of exotic flowers and flamboyants. Already Susan had set the servants to work, including Padstow whenever his inventive genius failed to think of an excuse, and in a few weeks, he knew, she would have produced order out of chaos. She could never remain idle for long.

'Roger.' She turned towards him and threw her bare arm across his chest. 'How long will you be gone?'

'A week, no more. I've no intention of pandering to Chandra Nath.'

'My brave Roger!' She turned so that her breasts, incredibly soft, rested on his body and her hand moved to his thighs. 'I know exactly how it will be. "What can I do for my English friends?" Chandra Nath will ask, his oily face all smiles. "Justice," says my Roger. "I demand you set free all those innocent Britons in Gheriah." "If only I could," the peshwa will say, raising his hands to heaven. "But they are pirates, you see, criminals over whom I have no control." '

She altered her voice so convincingly to imitate the Mahrattan leader and himself that Kelso could only laugh. 'Something like that, I dare say, in fact it's almost a waste of time to be going.'

'Then why go?'

'Because that's what the council wants, and, to be fair, there's something in their argument.' He hesitated and then added, with a grin, 'Besides, *Seahawk* won't be ready for a week.'

She laughed delightedly and pressed against him, smothering his face with kisses, until he was forced to make love. They were still locked in an embrace when Padstow knocked at the door.

They set off on the bund road in the early evening, Kelso in front with Pettigrew, who, to everyone's surprise, had insisted on making the journey, with Padstow and Kilgannon, a huge Scotsman, as escort in the rear. With the sun on their backs and their mounts still fresh they rode at a canter until twilight and camped in a clearing beside a stream for the night.

Of all possible travelling companions Kelso would have chosen anyone but Pettigrew, yet as he lay on his blanket, looking up at the myriad stars of heaven and listening to the rasp of cicadas and the croak of bullfrogs, he realized that this was an unexpected opportunity to talk. And to ask questions. Why had this foppish ex-member of council chosen to make this journey when he seemed the very last man to choose the heat and dust of the road? What would he be thinking now as he found himself forced to spend a night under the stars?

'Pettigrew, are you awake?'

'Yes, and shall be for most of the night, I shouldn't wonder, for it's too uncomfortable to sleep.'

'You'll sleep,' Kelso said, 'if only from tiredness. We must have ridden forty miles already.'

'My body would agree with you.'

'Something I've been meaning to ask you,' Kelso said. 'What happened on *Cleopatra*?'

There was a silence, and he heard Pettigrew turn to face him in the darkness. 'When the Mahrattans attacked? I don't know. I was below with the other passengers. Poor Abercrombie was hit, I imagine, by a sniper's bullet.'

'My wife doesn't think so. She was there when they brought him into the cockpit. His face was blown half away, she says, as though someone had shot him at close range.'

There was a long silence before Pettigrew answered. 'A remarkable woman, Lady Susan,' he said, 'to be such an expert. But if what she says is true isn't it possible that Abercrombie shot himself?'

'Why on earth should he do that?'

'I don't know, except that he would have had a lot to answer for if he'd survived.'

'How could he have known that? I thought he was killed before the battle was started.'

'Not entirely. There had already been some ranging shots. *Normandie* had a big gun in her bows, which was causing damage. *Rouen* was still half a mile away but closing fast.'

'You speak as though you saw it all.'

'What?'

'I thought you were below.'

Pettigrew was silent for a moment, and his answer when it came was loaded with what seemed a spurious anger. 'Damn you, Kelso! Is this an interrogation?'

'I'm only trying to find out what happened.'

117

'Why? Can't you accept what I told the governor?'

'It would be easier if it tallied with what I've heard from my wife.'

'She was below.'

'So were you, or have I misunderstood?'

'No. What I meant was she went down before me, she was so keen to organize the cockpit.' He added, 'Besides, she's a woman.'

'What has that to do with it?'

'We were going into action: you know, better than I what that means, the noise and the confusion. What woman could keep her wits in those circumstances and remember afterwards with any accuracy what happened?'

'Susan could.'

Pettigrew gave an audible sniff and leant back on his elbows. The moon was rising above the trees and one side of the glade was edged with silver. Across by the horses Kilgannon stood guard while Padstow snored to out-do the frogs.

'There will be a court of enquiry,' Kelso said. 'You realize that? On the face of it there was no reason why *Cleopatra* should have been lost.'

'Exactly! That's why Abercrombie may have taken his own life.'

'You think it was his fault?'

'It was his responsibility. He would certainly have been blamed.'

Kelso nodded. That was one of the penalties of command. When your ship was attacked you depended on your experience and skill and on the discipline of your crew, yet so much depended on luck. A single shot damaging one of the masts or the hull below the water line could signal defeat, while a more fortunate captain, fighting perhaps with less determination and skill, might bring his ship through unscathed.

118

'In any event,' Pettigrew continued, 'if you have a court of enquiry there will be precious few to give evidence.'

'*Seahawk* is in port. Her officers must have seen something.'

'From a distance of half a mile – probably more – and don't forget they were fighting their own action.'

'They might help to explain why the convoy made such poor progress.'

'I can tell you that.'

Kelso waited and then said, 'I didn't read that in your report.'

'No one asked me.'

'Or perhaps you thought we didn't know that the convoy should have been much farther west.'

'Hell's teeth, Kelso, have a care! It sounds as though you're blaming me for *Cleopatra's* misfortunes.'

'I'm only trying to find out what happened.'

'Very well. I'll tell you. Soon after you transferred to *Agamemnon* something went wrong with *Cleopatra's* steering.'

'Do you know what?'

'I'm no expert: in any case it would have been wrong for me to interfere, even though I was the senior Company man aboard. Could it have been the steering chains?'

'Perhaps. Can you describe what happened?'

'Easily. One moment we were sailing in good order, with *Protector* a quarter of a mile to larboard and another Indiaman, I've forgotten her name – '

'*Hooghli*?'

'That's right – *Hooghli* to starboard. Suddenly *Cleopatra* veered off course. I tell you, it was quite frightening. The ladies screamed, the captain swore and almost hit the quartermaster, the ship heeled over and, according to Abercrombie, if orders hadn't been quickly given and as quickly obeyed she might have broached to.'

119

'What happened then?'

'I don't know. I was below.' He hesitated. 'I had just gone below to see whether the violent turn had upset the furniture in my cabin. We hove-to and Abercrombie sent the carpenter below. It must have been something serious because we stayed like that for half the day. When we set sail again, just before nightfall, we were under headsails only and making no more than three knots.'

So that was how it had happened. Kelso could imagine Fenton's frustration as the whole convoy lay hove-to, with the burning sun overhead, the wind, or what there was of it, still ahead, and, somewhere beyond the horizon, the French and Mahrattan fleet drawing nearer. All this had happened within hours of taking command.

'Was *Cleopatra*'s steering put right eventually?' he asked.

'So it seemed. We sailed under reefed canvas through the night, but at dawn, or soon after, the enemy fleet was sighted.'

'And it was then that the steering failed again?'

'Yes, well not immediately. It happened when the French ship of the line was just coming into range. Although *Protector* had signalled the convoy to proceed in line of battle *Cleopatra* simply veered off to starboard, and Abercrombie was forced to fight the battle on his own – at least until *Seahawk* came to join her.'

'But by then Abercrombie was dead – and you think he blew his brains out?'

'I don't know, but it's the most likely explanation.'

'Not to me,' Kelso said. 'I knew Abercrombie. I served with him for a time on the old *St Helens*. He was a God-fearing man, a keen church-goer; he would never have taken his own life.'

'Well, he's dead: that's all we know.'

'And Tulliver,' Kelso said, 'although I doubt that he could have added much.'

'If you ask me,' Pettigrew said, 'we'll never know the truth. Abercrombie's dead, his crew are prisoners in Gheriah and Fenton on *Protector* is at St Helena.'

Kelso nodded in the darkness. 'You're right. For the moment we can only speculate. But there's one point on which I disagree. We'll get the truth, if not now, then later. I want to know, and so will the court of directors, how one of the newest Indiamen, carrying a valuable cargo was lost with all her crew and more than forty passengers. It doesn't make sense, and someone – perhaps the captured officers in Gheriah, or perhaps the carpenter – will know the answer.'

'If they are ever released from Gheriah,' Pettigrew said. 'We shall know more of that after we've seen Chandra Nath tomorrow.'

15

They crossed the river soon after noon at a ford, which now, towards the end of the monsoon, was high enough to keep the horses struggling, and came out on rising ground with high mountains to their left.

It was desperately hot. The sunshine, the swarms of midges which attacked horse and rider alike, and the warm, clammy air made riding a trial of strength and endurance and reduced conversation to an occasional query where the path divided and, from Padstow, the frequent oath.

They climbed steadily for most of the day and towards late afternoon came out on to a broad plateau. The mountains here were thickly wooded and cleft by deep ravines, the path, which had been scarcely more than a track through the long grass and scrub, suddenly developed into a well marked road. Villages appeared, and, for no apparent reason, since there was no other habitation in sight, a large temple. While the sun was still high, although shadows were lengthening, they were met by a troop of Mahrattan horsemen.

Kelso, with Pettigrew at his side, reined his horse to meet them.

'Salaam!' He raised his hand to their leader, a fellow with the hooked nose, thin lips and hard, relentless eyes of the Mahrattan warrior. 'We come to speak with the peshwa, Chandra Nath.'

'The peshwa sent for you?'

'My name is Kelso, commodore of the East India Company Marine. This is Sir Ralph Pettigrew, a senior member of council. The peshwa will see us.'

The leader stared at him angrily, as though more than ready to dispute his claim, but then, as Kelso rode forward, turned his horse aside. 'Follow me.'

They proceeded along the road, with the Mahrattan horsemen on either side and, after passing through several villages of almost unbelievable squalor, came out on to a maidan with the fort of Shanwar Peth and the sprawling town of Poona beyond.

The smell as they entered the narrow streets was nauseating, the stench of ordure and filth and decay. As they proceeded in single file, for there was not room between the buildings to ride abreast, they aroused great swarms of flies. Scrofulous children crawled about the street, ignoring the horses, and old crones sat in the doorways, watching the strangers pass. It was not until they reached the main square and turned westwards towards the river that they entered the area of the privileged.

The palace was on higher ground at the end of a broad, tree-lined street. There were sentries at the gate and, beyond, a lawn bright with flowering shrubs and shaded along its southern flank by trees. There were more sentries at the steps.

'These Englishmen seek audience with the peshwa,' the leader of the escort announced.

One of the sentries went inside and, after a long delay during which Kelso and his companions waited stoically in the sun, reappeared with a man they took to be an equerry.

'Sahibs! You wish to see my master?'

'Yes. Commodore Kelso and Sir Ralph Pettigrew of the Honourable East India Company, servants of His Majesty, King George of England.'

The equerry salaamed, acknowledging these credentials, and signalled them to enter.

Chandra Nath, the most powerful man in central India, received them in the throne room. He was not at all as Kelso had expected, for, unlike the sensuous and well-fed potentates of Bengal, he was spare of build, with the high, predatory nose of his people and eyes that were as keen and unrelenting as a hawk's. He looked from one to the other, but it was to Kelso that he addressed himself.

'You come with a message from King George?'

'We come on behalf of his subjects, those unfortunate men and women captured aboard the Indiaman *Cleopatra* and now imprisoned in Cowlapundi.'

'Ah, yes.' The peshwa motioned them to the cushions. 'A most regrettable incident.'

'An act of piracy, Your Excellency,' Kelso insisted, 'for which we, on behalf of His Majesty King George, demand retribution.'

The hooded eyes closed and the peshwa's voice took on a harder note as he replied. 'Demand? That is an unfortunate term, remembering that you have come alone, or almost alone, into the most important town of the Mahrattan kingdom.'

'We are Englishmen who came, relying on the honour of the Mahrattans. I cannot believe, Your Excellency, that a man of your distinction will find it necessary to use threats.'

'It is not I, commodore, who uses threats, it is not I who is demanding.' He smiled blandly, forcing Kelso on to a new tack.

'The Gherian pirates have been harassing the Company shipping for too long,' Kelso said. 'A few years back it was necessary to teach them a lesson.'

'Which will not be repeated, I trust,' the peshwa said, making no attempt now to veil his threat. 'What happened in Tulagee Angria's time is past, but not forgotten. Any repetition of that attack, even if unsuccessful, would be considered in Poona as an act of aggression.'

'Against whom, Your Excellency?'

'Against the Mahrattan people.'

'Then am I to understand that you condone these piratical adventures?'

'Certainly not. We are a civilized people who have been noted as warriors in the past and can still present the most powerful army in India, but who now wish for peace. We want good relations with all our neighbours, including the British.'

'Then would it be unreasonable to ask you to act against those Mahrattans who are disturbing the peace and making good relations impossible?'

The peshwa spread his hands and, for one disastrous moment, Kelso was reminded of Susan's impersonation as she lay naked on the bed. 'They are pirates, you see, criminals over whom I have no control,' Susan had suggested. 'They are beyond my control,' the peshwa said, 'pirates, criminals.'

'But you are strong. They would have no defence against a land attack,' Kelso said. He spoke hurriedly and forced a frown lest the Mahrattan leader should detect a smile.

Again the peshwa spread his hands. 'If only I could, but you have no idea, my friend, of the difficulties.'

'I can see none,' Kelso replied, coldly. 'Gheriah is by no means impregnable, even from the sea. By land, with this huge army of which you talk, it could be taken easily.'

The peshwa shook his head, obviously searching for an excuse, and then, unexpectedly, turned to Pettigrew. 'Sir Ralph, you see my position. How can I persuade my army to go to war against their own people?'

'Perhaps, Your Excellency, war is not necessary,'

Pettigrew suggested. 'If the Gherian pirates could be persuaded to suggest terms.'

The eagle profile softened with a smile. 'Ah, yes. I think that might be possible.'

'What kind of terms,' Kelso demanded, 'since you obviously know the minds of these criminals?'

The peshwa gave him a hard look. 'Have a care, commodore. Do not presume too far on my good will.'

'I am a man who values the truth, Your Excellency, as I am sure you are. Let us not bandy words. What are the Gherian terms?'

'Very well, since you want the truth: I think, my friend, that these pirates, as we will call them, would be happy to return the crew and passengers of *Cleopatra* and the cargo, which must be worth at least twenty lakhs, on one condition.'

'Which is?'

'That you and your company leave Bombay.'

Even Kelso, who was expecting some preposterous demand, was taken aback. 'You can't be serious!'

'Indeed I am. They say that would be a fair exchange for the lives of so many Englishmen.' He paused and added, as an afterthought, 'And Englishwomen.'

'The devil they do! And what about the factories, the fort, the fine houses that have been built, the dockyard?'

'Fair compensation would be given, naturally.'

'And what will happen to Bombay if we leave? Would you surrender it to the Gherians?'

The peshwa shrugged, as though surprised by such a naïve question. 'That would be open to negotiation.'

Kelso straightened his back and looked angrily at the Mahrattan leader. 'It is out of the question!'

'Then, I am sorry. I am afraid I cannot guarantee the safety of your people.'

'And I am sorry, Your Excellency, that I must now

resort to threats, whether you like it or not.' He leant forward. 'I give you fair warning that if one prisoner is harmed, just one, then England will make war on the Mahrattan people.' He held up his hand as the peshwa strove to speak. 'And if we made war it would not be with one battalion of Foot, not with a few thousand sepoys and the fighting ships of the East India Company Marine: it would be with the King's ships and the King's army and with an array of weapons which you can scarcely contemplate. We would destroy Poona, we would destroy this palace, we would overrun central India and subjugate the Mahrattan people.'

He had spoken quietly but with such force that even the peshwa was impressed. Only Pettigrew knew that he was bluffing and that he would have as much chance of persuading parliament to declare war on a remote Indian state as he would of becoming the next prime minister. But without a card in his hand he could only bluff.

'Perhaps, Your Excellency,' Pettigrew suggested, anxiously, for he was clearly worried by Kelso's forthrightness, 'perhaps the Gherian pirates would settle for something more reasonable.'

The peshwa sat in silence, staring straight ahead, but whether, overcome by Kelso's threat, he was considering a violent reaction, or whether, persuaded by his sincerity, he was wondering how far he should reduce his terms, was not clear.

'You will appreciate, Your Excellency, that when my friend the commodore speaks of threats he is speaking for London, which is many thousand miles away. He and I, in India, can see the problem on rather different terms.'

'We will settle for five crores,' the peshwa said, 'in gold and precious stones, the whole sum to be paid here, in Poona, before the prisoners are released.'

Kelso nodded, as one realist to another. 'It is a large

sum, Your Excellency, but not impossible. I will see what can be done.'

'Very well.'

'And since we are practical men I am sure you will see that we could only consider half the ransom in advance, the rest to be paid on the safe delivery of the prisoners.'

Again the peshwa considered. 'Very well.'

Kelso stood up. 'Then with your permission we will leave at once. I will let you have our reply within a week.'

The peshwa rose too and raised his hand in salutation. 'You are a brave man, commodore, a man after my own heart. I wonder how you can work with such fools as Raikes and Emmerson, or with Carew and Forster for that matter – when they are not sick. If you should ever think of leaving the Honourable Company – to make a fortune, for instance, before you return to England – let me know. I would be pleased to have a man like you in my administration.'

'In what capacity?' Kelso asked, with a hard smile. 'As commodore of your pirate fleet in Gheriah?'

16

The frigate *Seahawk* and *Agamemnon*, sloop of war, sailed out on the evening tide and headed north. The crew and most of the officers believed, as they had been told, that they were proceeding on a routine patrol. Only Kelso, who had taken over temporary command of *Seahawk*, and Cantwell of *Agamemnon* knew their true mission.

'We have only one course open,' Kelso had insisted, at a stormy meeting of the council. 'Chandra Nath has no intention of releasing the prisoners, even if we find the ransom.'

'Which we can't,' Raikes said, 'not without help from Fort William and Madras.'

'And the agreement of the court of directors in London,' Emmerson added, 'which might take months, possibly a year.'

'We can't wait that long,' Kelso insisted, 'even if we had any confidence in Chandra Nath's intent.'

'I disagree,' Pettigrew had argued. 'I think you've misjudged Chandra Nath. Five crores is a huge sum, I know, but is any price too high for the lives of so many Britons?'

Kelso had looked at him impatiently. '*If* – and I repeat, if – we could find such a huge sum and we had the means of transporting it to Poona, what guarantee have we that Chandra Nath would keep his side of the bargain? Do you believe that a man whose one ambition is to see the

British out of India is going to give up such a bargaining counter?'

'Certainly, if we pay his ransom.'

'Then you are more gullible than I thought, which surprises me after so many years in India. He will release some, perhaps two hundred, and hold the rest on some pretext – they are ill and therefore unfit to travel, or they have escaped and can't be found. And, believe me, the ones they fail to release would be the most important, some of the women, the children and the richer merchants. I tell you, gentlemen, I have no faith in any promise of Chandra Nath.'

So, reluctantly, and despite Pettigrew's objections, the council agreed to send an expedition south to Gheriah. The governor, who was in the wretched position of believing that Kelso was right but could not give whole-hearted support while he remained responsible for the lives and safety of all the Company servants in Bombay, was eventually persuaded by Kelso's assurance that Chandra Nath had taken heed of his threat that England would declare war if the prisoners were hurt or Bombay invaded.

With the council persuaded, Kelso's remaining difficulty had been Susan. She had not believed his tale of a routine patrol, especially at such a critical time in Bombay affairs, and she had demanded that if an expedition was going to Gheriah she should be included. Kelso had lied as convincingly as he knew how, and they had parted on distant terms.

The monsoon was nearly over, and the weather, capricious as a wilful woman, made sailing difficult. As they turned northwards, with the wind on their quarter, they were making eight knots, but as soon as they were out of sight of land and Kelso ordered canvas to be reduced to headsails and reefed courses, the wind swung away to the north-west, and, after an hour or more of sailing close-hauled, had reduced to the merest breeze, scarcely enough to give steerage way.

'We'll be beating to windward, sir, I reckon for the next few days,' Jones, the first lieutenant, said. 'The north-east trade is overdue.'

'You're right, only we shan't be beating against it, we'll have it on our quarter.'

Jones, who was an elderly man and rather slow in response, looked bewildered. 'How is that, sir? You mean we are changing course?'

'As soon as it's dark and we are far enough from land and free of any coastal traffic.'

It was almost dark already. The last resplendent colours of twilight were fading, and the horizon, which only moments ago had been a distant backcloth of reds and purples, was visibly shortening. A boy was coming aft to light the binnacle lamp.

'I am afraid we had to leave in some secrecy,' Kelso explained, 'and I'm sorry that it was not possible to tell you our real mission.'

'We are going south, sir,' Jones said, 'is that it? We are going to rescue those poor souls in Gheriah?'

'If we can.' He glanced at the first lieutenant as they leant side by side against the taffrail and was glad to see that there was no sign of resentment. 'I could not inform you earlier, but you will realize that our best, and, perhaps, our only chance lies in surprise.'

'I realize that, sir, and please don't be concerned on my account. In all my years in the service I've reckoned to do my duty to the best of my ability and to carry out any orders I've been given. So long as I know what's expected of me, sir, I'm quite content.'

Kelso smiled and nodded. 'Thank you, Mr Jones. I'm sure we shall get along famously.'

'The only thing is, sir,' Jones continued, after a long silence, 'aren't we taking rather long odds?'

'On the face of it, yes, but not if we achieve surprise. I intend to keep fairly close to the plan we used successfully a fortnight ago when we made another attempt.'

'Aye, sir. I've heard of that. Didn't *Agamemnon* sink two gallivats to block the channel?'

'Yes, and what she's done once she can do again.' He paused and, after looking landwards, said, 'But first I think we have done enough to confuse the trail. Alter course sou'-sou'-west, if you please.'

'Hands to braces! Hands to headsheets!'

As *Seahawk* turned before the wind and *Agamemnon*, receiving her signal, followed, the ship seemed to spring to life: the deck timbers, which had groaned protestingly as they beat to windward, suddenly adopted a more vibrant note, the decks, instead of tilting, first to starboard, then to larboard, took on a fore and aft motion as, with bowsprit rising and falling, *Seahawk* thrust into the waves. The sails were full, for the wind, capricious as ever, had strengthened at this, the first sign of the north-east trade, and with a line of phosphorescent wake cutting the darkness and a mist of spray reaching as far as the quarterdeck *Seahawk* set her bows southwards.

A quarter of an hour had passed before Jones rejoined Kelso at the taffrail.

'Plain sailing, sir,' he said, 'as long as this wind holds. We'll be off Gheriah in a couple of days.'

'That's what I hope. We'll keep well to westward, away from the shipping lanes, and pray that we shan't be seen. We'll come in at nightfall, with this wind, if it holds, on our beam. You'll drop me with fifty men – we'll call for volunteers tomorrow – to the north of the channel and in the lee of the headland. An hour before dawn you'll sail with *Agamemnon* and position yourselves on either side of the channel.'

'Assuming, of course, that we're not detected?'

'Whether you're detected or not don't matter. To catch the Gherians and, more important, the two French ships of war inside the harbour is what matters.'

'Won't they come at us, sir, at first light?'

'Probably, but so long as you and Cantwell keep your heads and the gunners their nerve you'll do what *Agamemnon* did alone a fortnight ago, you'll block the channel.'

Jones was silent for a time, not because of any misgivings, Kelso thought, but because he was a man who needed to consider slowly. 'The guns of the fort, sir, won't they be in range?'

'Yes, and they'll straddle you with a few salvos from time to time, I shouldn't wonder. It's a penalty you'll have to accept, although if you keep outside the channel you'll be at extreme range. Cantwell will arrange it so that one of you is always firing while the other turns. In that way you'll present moving targets while still maintaining your fire on the channel.'

'What shall we do, sir, when the channel's closed?'

'You will stay there, half a mile to sea, I suggest, to be out of range, but near enough to move in if the channel is cleared.'

'And *Agamemnon*?'

'Will sail in as close as she dares to a lee shore on the northern side of the headland where, if all goes well, I shall be waiting with my band of fifty and the prisoners.'

They proceeded south under all plain sail for a night and a day and the following night. On dawn of the second day they found themselves once again on a vast and empty ocean. Everything had gone well, too well Kelso felt, for he could not help thinking that sooner or later their luck must change. Coming on deck at dawn he returned the salute of young Travers, who had the watch, and, after glancing at the slate and traverse board, joined him at the weather rail.

'Another fine morning, sir, and a fair wind,' the young man said. 'We'll be off Gheriah by nightfall.'

'I hope so.' Kelso looked at the young, fresh face and wondered if ten or twelve years ago he had looked so innocent. Travers was more like a choir boy than a Marine officer, but he might still do well in action. 'Are you coming with me on the shore party?'

'Yes, sir, if you're agreeable.'

'Why not? We can do with some young blood. Have you been on a shore party before?'

'No, sir, but on *Surat* I was in charge of the gig on a cutting-out expedition.'

'Was it successful?'

'Yes, sir, although – ' The young man hesitated and blushed. 'Not on account of me, sir, I'm afraid.'

'What happened?'

'The first lieutenant in the longboat and the bo'sun in the cutter tied up without being seen and their parties went aboard. I was supposed to come in at the stern, but one of my men got drunk before we started and lost his oar. By the time we had rowed round the frigate a couple of times and before we could tie up it was all over. The ship was ours.'

Kelso laughed, pleased by the young man's honesty. 'Better to have it happen as a guinea pig than as a commissioned officer. You'll have a chance tomorrow, I hope, to distinguish yourself.'

'Sail ho! Sail on the larboard bow!'

The cry from masthead sounded with all the urgency of a warning bell. So near! If they were discovered now, only a day's sailing from Gheriah, all would be lost.

'What do you make of her?'

134

'There's two on 'em, sir, both hull down. All I can see are their topgallants.'

'How are they sailing?'

'Due north, sir, I reckon, although – ' He hesitated and not only Kelso but everyone on deck waited tensely 'One on 'em's changing course, sir. Must have seen us. Other one's following suit. Yes, sir, they're both heading this way.'

17

'Up you go, Tanner,' Kelso said, in as calm a voice as he could manage. 'Tell me what you see.'

He waited, hands clasped behind back, apparently calm, as the midshipman shinned up the rigging. On deck the crew crowded the starboard bulwark as though what could be seen only hull down from masthead and then with the aid of a glass could also be seen from deck level with the naked eye.

'What are those men doing, Mr Lovegrove?' he shouted, more to relieve his feelings than to express anger. 'Get them back to work.'

'Aye, aye, sir.'

If the two ships were Indiamen – and this was possible since with the French no longer in Pondicherry the Company might risk sending unescorted merchantmen eastwards – he could still hold to his plan, but the more he thought of the matter the less likely this seemed. The port commander at St Helena would not know that two French ships of war had joined the Mahrattans, although Fenton would soon be apprising him of the fact, and, following the usual sea lanes, these Indiamen, if such they were, would have passed within fifty miles of the Gherian coast. It was unlikely, to say the least, that they would have passed unobserved.

'Deck there!' came Tanner's shrill voice from maintop. 'They're ships of war, sir, just coming hull up.'

'What do you make of them?'

'They're Frogs, sir – I'll stake my life on it. One's a three-decker.'

'And the other?'

'Something smaller, sir. I reckon a frigate.'

Normandie and *Rouen*! So, within a day's sailing of Gheriah the French ships had come out to meet them. Gone was all hope of surprise, gone was the chance of rescuing the English prisoners.

'What are they doing, sir?' asked Jones, who had come on deck as he heard the shouting.

'*Normandie* and *Rouen*. Somehow – God knows how – they must have learnt our plans.'

'Does that mean we'll have to alter them, sir?'

'It means more than that,' Kelso replied, savagely. 'It means that we'll have to cancel them.'

'And return to Bombay?'

'After we've exchanged visiting cards.' Kelso went to the companion way and called, 'Mr Lovegrove! Beat to quarters, please, and clear for action.'

As the drum rolled and the watch below came tumbling out, encouraged by the cries and stinging rattans of the bo'sun's mates he considered the engagement ahead. It would be more politic, he knew, if there were no engagement at all, for, still some fifteen miles distant and with the weather gage, the English ships could alter course for Bombay and be over the horizon before the bigger French ships could follow. There would be no dishonour in retreat, although he knew how some jealous tongues, Pettigrew's for instance, would wag. But it was not this that deterred him, but rather an inbred arrogance, which came of the belief in English superiority as much as the memory of past success. He could not bring himself to run from a Frenchman.

On deck the crew were following the well-drilled routine, hoses had been rigged to pumps, decks were already doused and sanded, water buckets had been placed by guns and at the mainmast, the gunner's party were just emerging from the hold with powder and shot. Below, bulkheads were being knocked down, including the one in his own cabin, and Noakes, the surgeon, was in the cockpit supervising the moving of midshipmen's chests to make improvised beds.

'If she's *Normandie*, sir, a ship of the line, she'll be carrying heavy metal,' Jones suggested, as he joined Kelso at the wheel.

'Too heavy for us if she closes, even worse for *Agamemnon*. We'll just have to see that she doesn't close.'

'Aye, aye, sir. Then *Rouen* – well, she's European built, bigger than us and carrying twenty-four-pounders.'

'And made of oak,' Kelso reminded, 'which can't resist shot like Indian teak.'

Jones thought about this for a moment and then smiled. 'Aye, sir. That's right.'

Cargill, the quartermaster, was less easily persuaded and, having heard this exchange, allowed his saturnine expression to become even more pronounced. With his tall stooping figure bent like a question mark over the wheel he held *Seahawk* steady on course, but you could see that his heart wasn't in it.

'How long before we're in range, sir?' Jones asked.

'An hour, possibly more. You can stand down the watch below until we're nearer.'

It was an hour of tension for all on board, a tension which was not lessened by the fact that most had been through it before. Soon, when the ships were in range, the guns would open up, tons of deadly metal would go hurtling from one ship to another, frail flesh and bone would stand defenceless except for the illusory protection of the bulwarks, the skill of captain and helmsman, and, most importantly, luck. To think of being hit was the stuff of nightmares and best not contemplated, if that were possible, while the enemy drew ever nearer.

'*Normandie* has opened up,' Travers said, an hour later, as the ships approached in line of battle. His voice was not quite as steady as usual, Kelso noted, but thought none the less of him for that. Even the bravest could feel qualms at the approach of battle.

'With the long tom in her bows,' one of the midshipmen scoffed. 'Fat lot of good that will do her!'

Kelso agreed with the youngster's assessment although he could not afford to do so openly since he had no right to voice his opinions openly on the quarterdeck. The long barrelled nine-pounder fired at extreme range from the rising and falling foredeck was unlikely to hit anything by intent although the noise was thought by some captains to be good for morale. No one saw the splash, and before the shot could be repeated the two leading ships were manoeuvring for position.

With the weather gage, the immediate advantage was with the English. Kelso, leading in *Seahawk*, could pass to starboard or larboard and would hope to exchange two broadsides for *Normandie*'s one. Then, with the positions reversed and having attacked or avoided the following *Rouen*, he would have to wear ship, exposing for a time *Seahawk*'s vulnerable stern. It was a nice exercise in seamanship.

'Have those starboard guns ready, Mr Lacock!' Kelso shouted to the gunnery officer. 'Fire on my order!'

'Aye, aye, sir.' He could see Lacock kneeling by number seven gun, making sure, no doubt, that one gun at least would be laid to his satisfaction.

'Sir!' With the leading ships now on collision course and only a quarter of a mile apart the quartermaster was getting anxious.

'Hold her steady!'

'There's another one, sir, from her bow chaser,' Travers called, and, in a moment, they heard the shot whistle overhead.

'Let them wait, lads!' Kelso shouted to the gunners, who were clearly anxious to retaliate. 'We'll announce ourselves directly.'

'Sir!' Cargill was croaking again, seeing a collision imminent, and was startled out of his wits by Kelso's voice in his ear. 'Helm a-weather!'

'Hands to braces!'

As *Seahawk* spun to leeward with the wind on her quarter, yards were braced, keeping the canvas full, and as she shot at less than a cable's length across *Normandie*'s bows, Kelso shouted, 'Fire!'

The starboard guns roared out with well-drilled precision at the exact moment that the deck levelled. *Normandie*, clearly taken aback by this manoeuvre, received the full weight of metal in her bows and, with fo'c'sle shattered and holes showing above the water line, sheered off to starboard, exposing her larboard bow for *Seahawk*'s second broadside.

'Swab out! Reload! Take aim! Fire!'

Drill it was, which won battles, as Commodore James, his old mentor, had always maintained. A frigate, sailed by a well drilled crew, was always a match for the heavier metalled ship of the line. On *Seahawk*'s gundeck crews were already at tackles, while cleaners thrust their sponges into barrels, loaders waited with rammers, and the gun captains crouched fover breeches, ready to take aim and fire.

The deck crew, too, were waiting at sheets and braces, ready to implement without delay the captain's orders. As *Seahawk* turned before the wind and fired her second broadside Kelso knew that he need have no worries with this crew.

'Stand by to go about!'

Normandie was just firing her first broadside.

It came thunderously about their ears, three shots landing near the mainmast and one on the quarterdeck, while a fifth ploughed into the fo'c'sle head.

'Fire party forward! Get that wreckage cleared! Loblolly boys, see to the wounded!'

There were four, lying in grotesque positions by number three gun, which had received a direct hit. Although one had lost a leg and another was clearly dying, for the deck around him was running with blood, no one screamed or shouted for help. Those dreadful cries would come later when the surgeon started his grisly work in the cockpit.

'*Agamemnon*'s been hit, sir!' Jones cried.

He had almost forgotten the sloop-of-war, but he saw her now, clawing her way to windward, with the French frigate in pursuit. Her jibboom had been shot away and her headsails were trailing.

'Mr Lacock! Target *Rouen*. Fire as you bear!'

So intent was the French captain on the sloop that he clearly had no eyes for *Seahawk*. The two ships were beam-on, at a distance of less than a hundred yards when the Marine frigate fired her broadside.

Once again precision was perfect. The guns roared out together and, almost at once, so close were the ships, *Rouen* received the full impact.

She seemed to stop dead in her tracks. On the starboard tack, she lurched over so that with her deck tilting to larboard she was in danger of broaching to.

'Swab out! Reload! Fire!'

Again *Seahawk*'s guns roared out, and *Rouen*, desperate to escape, turned about and ran before the wind to safety.

In the meantime Lemarchand on *Normandie* had not been idle. As the huge ship of the line turned into the wind her starboard guns roared out, and *Seahawk*, straddled by thirty-two-pounders, heeled over and, as *Rouen* had done only minutes before, threatened to broach to.

'Hold her steady!' Kelso shouted to the quartermaster. 'Mr Lovegrove, see to those braces!'

Slowly the frigate righted herself and, despite the confusion on deck, where more dead and wounded by the larboard guns were being dragged away and the bo'sun, red-faced and hoarse with shouting, was detailing a party of waisters to clear the wreckage, Kelso shouted to the gunnery officer: 'Fire as you bear, Mr Lacock!'

The two ships were now sailing on parallel courses with *Seahawk* to windward and at a distance of less than a cable's length. Having just discharged a broadside, *Normandie's* starboard gun crews could be seen swabbing out and reloading; a broadside accurately laid now might be doubly effective.

Lacock no doubt realized this, for, despite the obvious impatience of his larboard gunners, who had suffered more than their share of casualties, he was running from gun to gun, checking over open sights that line and elevation were to his liking.

At last he seemed satisfied. Standing back by the mainmast he shouted, 'Fire!'

Synchronization was so perfect that *Seahawk* rocked back on her beam and the thunder of twelve eighteen-pounders, fired simultaneously, was like a single clap.

Immediately, as the guns recoiled to the extent of their breechings, crews were ready at train tackles, while loaders stood by with sponges, ladles and rammers, and the captains waited impatiently with spikes and quoign mallets to check line and elevation. No chance for them to observe the fall of shot, but a spontaneous cry from the deck crew told them that they had made several hits.

In fact, as Kelso saw, Lacock's patience had been well rewarded, for there were holes in the French ship's hull along the gundeck, and when she fired again, which she did almost immediately, it was a wild and inaccurate affair.

'One more, lads!' Kelso shouted to the larboard gunners. 'They won't forget *Seahawk* in a hurry.'

The deck crew and the larboard gunners cheered, while once again the barrels were carefully laid.

'Fire!'

The ships were even closer now, since *Normandie* was on the starboard tack, and it would have been difficult for even an inexperienced gunner to miss. *Seahawk*'s gunners were not inexperienced and they were still mad for revenge. Their broadside tore further holes in the Frenchman's hull, and one shot, less well directed than the rest, although in fact more effective, broke the mizzen topgallant yard.

'Wear ship!'

As *Seahawk* turned, still clinging to the weather station, *Normandie*'s guns fired into her stern but, weakened and dispirited by the constant pounding, their crews did little damage.

'Look, sir!' Jones called. '*Agamemon's* in a bad way.'

The sloop-of-war, without her jibboom and with an ominous tear from tack to leech in her mainsail, had lost the only advantage she had over these much bigger vessels: she had lost manoeuvrability and speed. *Rouen* was again coming into the attack.

'Four points to starboard,' Kelso ordered. He could not leave *Agamemnon* to her fate.

Rouen's captain, who had been coming in hopefully for the kill, suddenly realized that the English frigate was looming up to starboard. He changed course, hoping to get in a position where he would be shielded by the sloop-of-war, but Cantwell was obviously alive to this, for *Agamemnon*, by changing course into the wind, forced her to meet the English frigate.

They were two ships evenly matched. *Rouen*, the heavier ship – for the term 'frigate' bore different meanings in European and Indian shipyards – also had the advantage of twenty-four-pounder guns, but *Seahawk* had the advantage of a superbly trained and disciplined crew and a commander whose experience of naval warfare was second to none.

'Stand by the starboard guns!' Kelso called, as calmly as if this had been a commodore's exercise. 'Stand by sheets and braces!'

The two ships approached on collision course, but Cargill, more appreciative now of the commodore's skill, remained silent.

'Starboard your helm!'

The wheel spun, yards were braced, and as *Seahawk* shot down the side of the French frigate her starboard guns roared out at almost point blank range, smothering any effective reply.

The ships cleared and, having lost the weather gage, *Seahawk* turned into the wind. Now, if the French captain kept his head, it would be the Marine vessel which would be pounded.

But to Kelso's surprise and irritation *Rouen* disclaimed the advantage. With the wind on her quarter she pulled away, following *Normandie*, which as Kelso now saw, was already half a mile to leeward.

'They've had enough, sir!' young Travers shouted. 'The Frogs have had enough.'

It was true. Although both French ships had taken a pounding neither was damaged sufficiently to call off the action.

Yet, Kelso thought, bitterly, as he watched them making the horizon, they had achieved what they had set out to do. They had thwarted his plans to rescue the prisoners from Gheriah.

18

'So it was a fiasco!' Pettigrew said. 'We've shown our hand, Chandra Nath has been warned and will no doubt be raising his price if we don't pay soon.'

'If we don't capitulate, you mean,' Kelso replied. 'I'm sorry, Pettigrew, but that's not the way to act. The Indians respect strength.'

'Which we patently lack.'

'And force: they've a healthy regard for force.'

'My dear Kelso, a frigate and a sloop-of-war, both unfortunately damaged, a battalion of Foot and a few thousand sepoys: is that what you call force?'

'*Normandie* and *Rouen* were damaged too.'

'The truth is,' the governor said, clearly anxious to stop this quarrel before it started, 'that we were unlucky. Because the French ships of war happened to be patrolling that stretch of the ocean – '

'No!' Kelso beat his hand on the table. 'They didn't *happen* to be there. Where we met them was well out of the normal lanes of patrol.'

The members of council watched him uneasily, wondering, perhaps, why it was always Kelso who voiced their hidden fears. The air was stifling in the council chamber, for it was not long after noon, and it said much for their appreciation of the dangers of the situation that the meeting had been called in this, the hottest part of the day. Raikes was there, looking even more drawn than usual, Emmerson was visibly wilting as he leant fat arms on the table. Carew, who had recovered from his bout of fever, had also been persuaded.

'You mean they had been warned?' the governor said.

'I'm sure of it. The French ships wouldn't patrol together, they'd go out singly with their escort of gallivats. Somehow – I don't know how – they knew that we were coming. All they had to do was intercept.'

There was an uneasy silence while the members of council looked at their hands, at the table, where flies were already settling on the empty glasses, at the ceiling, where the punkah was slowly moving, but not at each other. Only Pettigrew seemed to endorse Kelso's view.

'Kelso's right. I mean, it's obvious. They *knew*.'

'But how?' The governor looked at him without much favour, for in all his years in office he had worked on the assumption that there were some things best left unsaid. 'No-one knew except those of us in this room.'

'Not me,' Carew protested. 'I was in bed.'

'That's right. Well, the rest of us, Emmerson, Raikes and myself.'

'And Pettigrew,' Kelso said.

'And you,' Pettigrew replied.

Kelso shrugged. 'It's hardly likely that I'd put my own expedition in jeopardy.'

'Not intentionally, of course, but a careless word – I expect we've all been guilty of it at times.'

'Not with a secret like this, I hope,' the governor said, primly.

'I told no-one,' Kelso said, firmly. 'I spoke to no-one outside this room.'

'Not even your wife?' Pettigrew was smiling as he said it, but the smile was tinged with malice.

'To no-one,' Kelso insisted. It was true, of course, yet he could not prevent a feeling of doubt. It was Susan herself who had raised the matter, guessing with womanly intuition, that this was no time for a routine patrol. The more she had insisted the more stubbornly he had denied, and yet – he acknowledged it to himself – he was a poor liar. Could she have betrayed him, as she betrayed him in Bengal, thinking quite honestly, he was sure, that she was acting in his best interests? She was a strange, wilful woman, yet, despite all her faults, he loved her still.

'If someone spoke out of turn,' the governor said, 'and I think it far from proven, for we all know the kind of gossip that gets about the waterfront – but if someone spoke carelessly I hope that he will have learnt his lesson.' He looked round the table and said, firmly, 'Now I think we should waste no more time on speculation.'

'I agree,' Pettigrew said, 'for we have more important matters to consider: how quickly, for instance, we can raise the ransom and how we intend to transport such a weight of gold and precious stones to Poona.'

Kelso banged his fist on the table so firmly that poor Emmerson, who had been dropping off to sleep, woke with a start and the khitmutgar, thinking he had been summoned, showed his face at the door. 'You're wrong,' Kelso insisted, 'even to think of a ransom. If Chandra Nath wins now it will be the first nail in our coffin. He'll step up his demands, convinced of our weakness, and never rest until we are out of Bombay.'

'So you say!' Pettigrew retorted, 'but I think you are wrong. I think we should trust Chandra Nath.' He appealed to the others round the table. 'In any event, what choice do we have? No-one, I suppose, believes that we should leave the prisoners to the Mahrattans. They must be rescued somehow: perhaps Kelso will tell us what he proposes.'

'Certainly.' Kelso leant forward at the table and said, 'I think we should send another expedition – tonight.'

'Tonight!' Even the governor, who had heard a good

many of Kelso's plans over the years, was surprised. 'With what? *Seahawk* and *Agamemnon* are out of action, *Malabar* is on patrol. There are only the bomb ketches.'

'I'll take *Seahawk*,' Kelso said. 'She's damaged, but not so badly that she can't put to sea. The Mahrattans won't be expecting us, especially with *Normandie* and *Rouen* damaged.'

'But how?' The governor spread his hands. 'What will you do?'

'We'll sail tonight,' Kelso said, 'after dark. With the wind in our favour we can be off Gheriah within two days.' He looked round, clenching his fists, as he said, 'Surprise is what we need, gentlemen, and this is one way of achieving it. We'll land at Kalewa, north of the headland, and with a shore party of only fifteen or twenty we'll make our bid. It's a chance, perhaps a long chance, but I believe we should try.'

They were all silent, and it was a full minute before the governor said, 'Well, Kelso, like most of your plans it has the merit of boldness. I don't know whether you realize the odds against you – personally I think they are immense. On the other hand, we've no alternative – except, that is, to pay the ransom – so, if you gentlemen are agreed – '

They nodded, reluctantly it seemed, but then, as though gaining some of Kelso's confidence, began to smile. 'Good luck, Kelso. If you succeed – ' Only Pettigrew remained silent.

Kelso returned to his house and shouted for Padstow, who, to his indignation, was obeying Susan's orders to clean the sitting room. 'Belay that nonsense!' he ordered, as his steward came in wearing an apron and an aggrieved expression. 'Pack my sea chest. We're going to sea.'

'Praise be!' Padstow exclaimed, putting hands together and raising his eyes to the ceiling. 'Just shows, sir, that if you're a clean-living, God-fearing man like me your prayers are sometimes answered.'

'What's this?' Susan asked, as she came in carrying a list of jobs to be done. She smiled as she saw her husband and kissed him lightly on the cheek. 'You're not off again?'

'I'm afraid so.'

'Oh, Roger! You've only just returned.'

'Yes, but this is urgent.'

She looked at him closely, embarrassing him with her scrutiny. 'You're going to Gheriah.'

'No.'

'Roger!' She came and took his arms, forcing him to look at her, 'You tried to fool me once. It won't work again.'

'Why are you so interested?'

'Because if it's an attack on Gheriah you're planning I want to come.'

'Why?'

She shrugged. 'Conscience perhaps. I can't bear to think of all those prisoners, especially the women and children, living under intolerable conditions. Besides, I was a prisoner there myself. I know where they were held.'

He walked with her to the window and looked down, over a lawn and a semi-circle of beds which displayed a pathetic show of flowers, to the road and a stretch of open land beyond. An English soldier was there with a young Indian girl – she could not have been more than twelve. Her sari was open and he was caressing her brown body, her small, scarcely formed breasts, her waist, her thighs.

'Roger!' Susan clasped her arms about him and pressed herself against his body. 'Before you go – '

'No.' He pulled away. 'I must be off. We sail at dusk.'

'Another three hours.'

149

'There's a lot to do.'

'Roger!'

She could bend him almost effortlessly to her will: he acknowledged it and was ashamed, yet he knew that while she was with him it would always be so. As he held her in his arms and responded to her passionate embrace he could not forget that someone had betrayed their previous expedition. Could it have been Susan? Who knew what unholy alliance she might have formed while she was a prisoner, with only her beauty and her ruthlessness to save her?

And yet, he remembered hopefully, it was she who, without any sign of regret, had killed Bedi Roy.

'Darling!' She traced the line of his chin with her fingers and then drew him into a kiss. Her body was firm and shapely, more so than the Indian girl's they had just seen, and she had a way of love-making which made him forget all doubts and troubled thoughts, so that for a few minutes at least he was carried away beyond the restraints of caution. 'Darling, take me with you.'

Still clasping her in his arms he looked down into her eyes. 'No, it's not possible.'

'Why not?'

'Because I love you and I can't bear to think of you being hurt.'

'I shall be more hurt if you leave me behind.'

He looked down at the smooth skin of her shoulder and, moved by a sudden impulse, kissed the soft line of her neck. 'Why do you want to come?'

'I told you – because I have a conscience. I feel I owe it to those others who were left behind.'

'Do you think that you could help?'

'I'm sure of it. I *know* the fort, I know the way into the prison.'

'So do I. I've been there, too, remember.'

She shook her head. 'To the main gate, which is always guarded. You'll never get in that way.'

'There's another gate at the rear.'

'Which is equally difficult.' She put her hands on his shoulders and pleaded, 'Roger, take me – please! Alone, you'll stand no chance, with me you'd have every chance.'

He looked at her thoughtfully. 'You mean, you know some other way into the prison?'

'Yes.'

'Then tell me about it. There's still no need for you to come.'

'I must, Roger. I must.'

There was something he couldn't understand, something she was afraid to tell, yet she seemed to be sincere. 'Where is this secret entrance? At least tell me.'

She hesitated and, most improbably, for he could not remember that it had ever happened before, she blushed. 'It's a passage,' she said, 'leading from the western wall. It's unguarded and only barred by a rickety gate.'

'Where does it lead?'

She hesitated on a lie and then, clearly deciding to risk the truth, said, 'To Bedi Roy's bedroom.'

19

They anchored a cable's length from shore and rowed across the calm waters of the bay. There were still two hours to dawn, long enough, Kelso thought, to reach the town if they could find a path across the tidal marshes and to return, still in darkness, before the Mahrattans attacked. Success depended on certain premises, as he realized only too well. Sitting beside Susan in the stern sheets and watching the silent, palm-fringed beach draw nearer he hoped that the Mahrattans, lulled into a false sense of security by the recent sea encounter, would be caught by surprise, or if, as he suspected, they had been warned by the unknown traitor, they would be waiting at Kalewa, on the other side of the bay. He had told no-one of his change of plan until the last moment, not even Susan.

'It looks quiet enough, sir,' Travers whispered, showing as he turned the uncertainty in his eyes and in the tremulous movement of his lips.

Kelso nodded and smiled. Nerves before action were natural, he thought: the young man would be brave enough when the fighting started.

'Almost too quiet,' Susan whispered back. 'It makes me feel that we should be taking a moonlight stroll across the maidan.'

It was remarkable, Kelso thought, how she seemed to be entirely without fear. Her clear-cut profile and the firm set of her chin were as pronounced as if she had been taking tea with the governor's lady.

'I'll run her on to the beach, sir,' suggested Steel, the coxswain. 'Can't see any rocks.'

'If you please.'

They watched tensely, hands on cutlasses and pistols, as the keel ran smoothly into the sand. There was no movement, no sudden volley of shots, no sound at all apart from the rustle of palm fronds and the familiar croaking of frogs.

So far so good. After the crew had shipped oars and then, with cutlasses at the ready, spread out along the beach Kelso went forward and, standing ankle deep in water, turned to swing Susan to the sand. For a moment as he held her in his arms she clung to him and whispered, 'Good luck!'

'Two men to guard the longboat,' Kelso ordered. 'Mr Travers, take six men with you and see if you can find the track.'

Only minutes before, as they were rowed across the bay, he had cursed the moonlight, but now on what seemed a deserted and trackless beach he was glad that it would help them to get their bearings.

Beyond the palms and a tangle of undergrowth the marshes began, desolate and empty of water at the low tide, apart from streams which curved and eddied across the mud. They might have spent precious minutes or even longer searching for a track, but in fact, so clear was the moonlight, they saw at once a bund path crossing towards the town.

'There you are, lads,' Kelso said. 'We're in luck. Mr Travers will lead, Mr Steel will bring up the main party. And remember, if you value your lives, we want absolute silence.'

There had been no need to warn them, he thought, for they had all been picked especially for this operation. If they should be killed or captured the Marine would be that much the poorer. But he could not afford to think of failure.

They proceeded in file across the desolate marshland, seeing nothing except the fort across the bay and, almost directly ahead, the few lights of Gheriah, and hearing nothing except the rush of water signalling the turn of tide and the flapping wings of sea birds. They halted a quarter of a mile from town.

'Can you see it?' Kelso asked, quietly, as with his hand on Susan's arm he led her to the head of the column.

'Yes.' She pointed to a jetty, only a short way along the front, where a gallivat, larger and more ornate than the rest, was tethered. 'That is Bedi Roy's.'

'You know the way from there?'

'Yes.'

She went forward without waiting for him, and he was forced to lengthen his stride.

A whole mass of shipping was visible now, the masts as numerous as pins in a cushion; perhaps fifty to sixty grabs and gallivats were there, at least three merchantmen, victims of the Mahrattan pirates, and, in deeper water, the two French ships of war. There was no sign of a sentry.

They came upon him when they were least expecting it, a Mahrattan dozing against an upturned boat with a musket across his knees.

'What – ?' He was still half asleep as he struggled to his feet, but before he could raise his gun or shout Padstow had dispatched him with his knife.

The silence was eerie and unnerving. As they trod carefully along the stone-paved front, keeping wherever possible to the shadows, they passed a row of hovels, probably fishermen's huts, a warehouse and a fairly extensive boatyard: but no Mahrattans. Were they really asleep, Kelso wondered, or was this all part of an elaborate trap? It seemed incredible that there should not be one Mahrattan awake along the whole waterfront.

'This is it.' Susan had stopped by the quay and was pointing to the right where a narrow path led upwards through an opening in the wall.

Motioning her to silence, Kelso went forward.

The path rose steeply and unevenly over a base of shale and loose rocks and seemed at times to be almost impassable, so close were the sides and so dense the overhanging creepers, but Kelso pushed on until he came to a high wall.

It rose above him, sixty feet into the night sky, and was marked, as he now saw, by barred apertures which could have been windows and was topped by crenellations. They had come to the prison wall.

He turned to Susan, who was still climbing. 'Where now?'

She stopped with one hand on her knee and pointed.

He saw, when he pulled aside the creeper, the rickety gate she had mentioned and realized as he leant against it that it was unlocked. Indeed, it seemed so fragile that a good kick would probably have sent door and jamb crashing to the ground, but he could not afford such extravagant gestures now. He edged it open with his shoulder and stepped into a garden.

There was an open window, covered as he discovered in a minute by gauze, and he heard someone in the room beyond turning on a couch.

'Who's there?' a man's voice called, irritably, in Mahrattan.

Drawing his sword, Kelso stepped forward into the hanging gauze.

For a moment he struggled, caught by arms and feet, and he heard the man rising angrily from his couch. 'Who's there?'

155

With one arm free, and fearful lest the alarm should be raised, Kelso drew back his sword and plunged blindly forwards. By good fortune it struck the man through the chest, and he died, still spitted by the sword, at Kelso's feet.

'Bedi's brother, Hamid,' Susan said, calmly, as she stepped over the prostrate body into the room.

'Where now?'

'Come. I'll show you.'

He held her arm while the rest of the party gathered in the garden and only when he saw Steel raise his hand did he signify his readiness to follow.

She led him through the room and into a passage and into a larger room which smelt of flowers and incense and was littered as he soon discovered, following her in the darkness, with carpets and cushions and low tables.

'Wait!' He reached forward and held her arm. 'We need a light.'

'Over here.' She felt her way carefully to the side of the room, with which she was plainly familiar, and in a moment struck a flint to light a taper. There were several candles in holders about the room, and he thought as she lit them that she could not have been calmer if she had been welcoming night visitors to their home in Loll Diggy.

'Here.' She held up a lantern. 'We shall need this.'

It was not until they had left the private apartments and had proceeded to the main part of the prison that they encountered the first Mahrattans. At first the stone corridors were empty, but as he trod carefully forward, shielding the lantern with his arm, Kelso heard, or thought he heard, movement ahead. He stepped quickly to the wall and motioned Susan and the others to follow. The sentries – there were two of them – were talking idly, stopping every few paces, obviously unaware of danger: it was not until they turned the corner and felt strong arms round their throats and the death thrust in their sides that they knew that they were not alone.

'How much farther?' Kelso asked.

'Along here.' Susan pointed. 'To the end of the passage and across a courtyard.'

It seemed much lighter as they stepped out into the courtyard, but whether this was because of the rising dawn or the waning moon he could not tell. He remembered that even after they had found the prisoners they had to get them to the beach.

'Over here!'

Susan led round the edge of the courtyard, past a fountain which filled the night air with coolness and some steps which led down to the dungeons.

'Poor devils!' Kelso muttered. 'Is this where they are held?'

'There's worse below,' Susan replied. 'Prepare for shocks.'

It was the smell rather than the occasional cries and groans and the one prolonged scream which filled them with horror. Rising from the dungeons came the stench of excrement and urine, of sweating bodies and filth. Voices called to them as they descended, feeble cries for water, mercy and help, intermingled with a few defiant shouts. Against the barred door a prisoner – he could not recognize him as an Englishman – clung like a figure from hell.

'Merciful heavens! Are these from *Cleopatra*?'

His exclamation, in English, brought an incredulous silence to the cell. But only for a moment. Someone – he was clearly a sailor and an officer from the cut of his filthy uniform – came crawling to the bars and, reaching out with a emaciated arm, cried, 'Thank God! The English are here. Thank God!'

157

At once they were all there, one, two hundred men, women and children, crawling, leaping, shouting, screaming, weeping.

'Mr Travers!' Kelso shouted. 'Take your men above and watch out for attack.' He turned and caught the coxswain by the shoulder and shouted to make himself heard. 'Mr Steel, you go with half a dozen men – you'd best include Padstow – Find the guardroom and settle with the guard. Then bring me the keys.'

As the two parties hurried away and, in a few minutes, according to the shouts and oaths and sounds of clashing steel, encountered Mahrattan opposition, he held up his hands to speak.

'Quiet!' he shouted. 'Listen to me! Some of you – most of you – know me. I am Commodore Kelso. In a few minutes you will be free.'

They cheered, and some, who seemed too weak to stand, fell weeping to the ground. One lady, whom he remembered well, although he could not recall her name, knelt with mouth open, tears streaming down her face, and her hands clasped in prayer. The children, who had probably been cosseted by their elders' despite the terrible conditions, seemed stronger than most.

'When this door is opened,' Kelso went on, 'we shall have to move, and move fast. The frigate *Seahawk* lies hove-to no more than a mile from here.'

'But, commodore,' an old lady cried, 'we are weak.'

'I know, but we shall manage, we shall have to manage.'

'Some are too weak to stand.'

'We have some strong arms to support you,' Kelso promised. 'Those who are too weak to move will be carried. The rest will have to help each other, for, remember, we may not have much time.'

It was Padstow who brought the keys, a Padstow with knife arm red to the elbow and a broad grin on his face.

'Here you are, sir. Didn't want to part with them, they didn't, but we persuaded them.'

As the huge iron door swung open the prisoners stood for a moment as though dazed, or perhaps unable to believe their good fortune, until one – it was the officer in the bedraggled uniform – offered his arm to the nearest lady. 'Madam, may I have the pleasure?'

They surged out then, still shouting and weeping, but half a dozen remained prostrate on the ground. 'Mr Travers, let me have some of your men.'

They went in reluctantly, trying to mask their disgust as they trod through the filth, and five of the very sick were carried outside. The sixth, an old man whose face still seemed to wear an expression of welcome, was dead.

'Keep together now,' Kelso called. 'If we all help the weakest and keep going we should be on board *Seahawk* within the hour.'

Travers came up to him as they moved down the corridor. 'How did you get on?'

'I can't make it out, sir. We had to deal with perhaps twenty Mahrattans, no more. The place seems deserted.'

Kelso nodded as he put his arm round an old lady who was struggling to keep up. 'They've guessed wrong, or perhaps they were misinformed, for I'll wager that they are out in force at Kalewa.'

They were crossing the big room where the candles were still burning before he realized that he had lost Susan. She had been with him at the cell door but must have disappeared while he was talking to the prisoners. 'Mr Travers,' he called. 'Have you seen my wife?'

'No, sir. She didn't come with us. I thought – '

'Mr Steel. Have you seen my wife?'

'No, sir.'

'I seen her, sir,' called Padstow, who was carrying two

children, one on his back, the other, a girl of five, in his arms.

'Which way did she go?'

'This way, sir, the way we came.'

'Well, where is she? There's only this room.'

'And the bedroom sir. Perhaps – '

Padstow stopped as Susan appeared in the corridor. She was still smiling and quite unperturbed and she held a large casket in her arms.

'Susan! Where have you been?'

'My hard-won earnings,' she said, 'all the money I was taking home from Calcutta. The Mahrattans stole it, and Bedi Roy hid it in his room.' She smiled at her husband and said, 'Now you see why I had to come?'

20

It took longer to cross the marshes than he had hoped, and dawn had broken fully as the first contingent of prisoners was ferried to *Seahawk*. Two more had died on the way, and one young woman – he never did discover her name – had such a fit of hysterics that she had to be rendered unconscious before she could be carried to the beach.

But most of the emaciated passengers and crew from *Cleopatra* behaved admirably. Few were well enough to walk at more than the slowest pace, yet, supporting each other with their own weary bodies, they dragged themselves along the quay and out by the bund path. When they reached the beach they collapsed.

Susan, he was glad to see, gave all her support. Although hampered by the casket, which she insisted on carrying, she still managed to support a small child and to give a helping hand and words of encouragement to those that faltered.

The cutter and the gig had been lowered away to join the longboat, and before long the crowd of wretched humans on the beach had been reduced to a dozen. Kelso knew that the next trip would be the last.

They had been pursued, although half-heartedly, by a score of Mahrattans, but the real threat, as he saw only too clearly, would come from the sea. Already thirty to forty grabs and gallivats were twisting and turning through the channel.

'Well done, sir!' Jones welcomed him at the entry port. 'We've accommodated them as best we can in the cockpit and the main cabin. Some we've had to put in the 'tween decks, and those that are weakest – '

'Later,' Kelso said, with a smile. 'I'm glad you've done your best for them, but now we'll have to leave them to Noakes and his assistants and any spare waisters he can muster. We're not clear yet.'

As he spoke he pointed to the mouth of the channel where already a number of gallivats had emerged into the open sea. Following, like a moving snake, was a whole line of Mahrattan vessels, looking strangely beautiful with their lateen sails caught by the early sun.

'Make sail, Mr Jones, if you please.'

'Aye, aye, sir.'

'What course, sir?' the quartermaster called.

'Course sou'-sou'-west.' Too many Mahrattan vessels had escaped the trap for an assault on those still in the channel to be feasible. Like a horse threatened by wolves *Seahawk* could only run.

'You'll hope to shake them off, sir?' Jones asked, as he rejoined Kelso at the weather rail.

'If we can. I'm not sure that we can do it, for with a following wind they can show a fair turn of speed.'

He moved aft to the stern rail and through his glass saw more and more Mahrattan vessels joining the pack. The one piece of luck *Seahawk* had enjoyed was that the vessels in the channel had precluded the guns of the fort from opening up.

'Look, sir, in the harbour! Isn't that *Normandie* making sail?'

It was, and *Rouen* too. Even as he watched, the two French ships of war gathered way and made for the channel. Whatever damage they may have suffered in the recent action Lemarchand clearly thought that they would be useful weapons in what might prove to be the final battle against the British.

'Mr Lovegrove!' Kelso shouted. 'Rig out the boarding nets, if you please.' If the Mahrattan vessels showed the turn of speed he feared it would not be long before one or more grabs were lashed alongside.

'Mr Tanner,' he said, to the midshipman of the watch. 'Take a working party and bring some shot – half a dozen each will do, to starboard and larboard. Lodge them in the scuppers and make sure that they are properly secured.'

'Aye, aye, sir.' The midshipman hesitated. 'Beg pardon, sir, but won't the gunners – ?'

'These are not for the guns. You'd better make that clear. We'll need them if we have to repel boarders.'

He looked astern and saw that the leading gallivats were coming up fast. He could even see the swarthy faces of the Mahrattans and their white burnous and the curved knives at their belts.

'Beg pardon, sir. I'm sorry to trouble you – ' It was Noakes, sleeves rolled to the elbow and his white shirt stained with blood.

'What is it?'

'One of the passengers, sir, a young lady. She's wreaking havoc below, screaming and attacking everyone. She's plainly lost her reason.'

'Then quieten her, Mr Noakes – as mercifully and effectively as you can.'

'Aye, aye, sir.' The surgeon hesitated. 'Excuse me, sir, but Lady Susan said – '

'Well?'

'That if she could use your cabin she'd look after the poor female. I thought, if you were agreeable – '

'Of course. Carry on.'

'Sir!' It was Jones again, shouting as he pointed to

starboard. 'They're outpacing us, sir, by more than two knots. Before long we'll be surrounded.'

Kelso nodded. 'Then we must be ready for them.' He went to the companion way and shouted to the gunnery officer. 'Mr Lacock, are your guns ready?'

'All ready, sir.'

'Target gallivat coming up to starboard. Fire as you bear.'

'Aye, aye, sir.'

Never had he wished so strongly for a broadside to be effective. With the whole pack at their heels it was essential to strike an early blow.

Lacock must have thought so too, for he was hurrying from gun to gun, checking over open sights and making minor adjustments with spikes and mallets where an aim was not to his liking.

At last he was satisfied.

'Ready! Fire!'

Seahawk rolled to larboard as sixteen guns roared out as one, and for a moment the whole deck area was covered with a choking pall of smoke. Then a spontaneous cheer rang out as the gallivat received the full weight of metal fired from almost point blank range. Her hull was pitted with holes, her mast, with sail flapping, strained aft against a severed stay.

'Larboard guns ready!'

However gratified Lacock might be he had not forgotten that other Mahrattan vessels were coming to larboard.

'Take aim! Ready! Fire!'

Again *Seahawk* rolled with the impact and again the gunners were rewarded by the sight of a gallivat reeling under the damage.

But, as Kelso knew, the pack was not likely to be deterred by the destruction of its leaders. More gallivats were coming up fast, and a grab, creeping in unnoticed,

164

was already securing grapnels to the mainchains.

'Mr Tanner!' Kelso shouted. 'We've a visitor to larboard. Make sure she's welcome.'

'Sir?'

It was unfair, he realized, to expect the boy to know what he had to do, and he ran down the companion to the maindeck and, using all his strength, picked up one of the eighteen-pound shots. 'Here, I'll show you.'

Moving forward and cheered on by the crew, who were proud of their eccentric commodore, he hoisted the shot on to the bulwark and, after pausing a moment to regain his breath, rolled it over the side.

It dropped like a plummet and went straight through the deck boards of the grab like a knife through butter. There were cries from below and some of the Mahrattans clustered round with rope and canvas as they tried to stem the inrush of water. 'There you are, lad,' Kelso said. 'Another like that and they'll be too busy to come aboard.'

But these successes were relatively unimportant. He knew that as he hurried aft. You could stop or discourage two, three, even a dozen Mahrattans, but there were always more to take their place.

Then as he reached the quarterdeck he was almost blown off his feet by a shot which cut through the mizzen shrouds, ploughed across the deck, only missing the lugubrious Cargill by inches, before plunging through the stern rail into the sea. The gallivats were opening up with their six-pounders.

'Sir! There's another one alongside, making fast to the starboard chains.'

'Very well. Young Tanner will know what to do.' The trouble was that the deck guns could not be depressed sufficiently to deal with a grab lashed alongside. Before long there might be half a dozen, snapping and snarling at their heels.

'Keep her steady, Mr Cargill!' he called, as *Seahawk* veered to starboard.

'Doing the best I can, sir,' the quartermaster replied, 'but we're carrying so much weight, dragging these blasted grabs, that it ain't easy.'

'Do the best you can.'

He wondered how Noakes was getting on below and whether Susan had succeeded in calming the mad woman. He wondered whether any of the last Mahrattan broadside had struck below the waterline, for even a six-pounder could do considerable damage. He wondered how much longer they would be able to keep going with the pack still at their heels.

'Look, sir – coming up astern!'

As he turned, following Jones' warning, he felt dismay, verging on despair. Bitterness, too, he felt, that all their efforts, the two expeditions, the night trek across the marshes, the rescue of the prisoners and their painful transport to the beach, had been in vain. *Normandie* and *Rouen* under all plain sail were coming up astern.

'What will you do now, sir?' Jones asked. 'Will you strike?'

'Never!' Not once in his long, venturesome career had he yielded while his ship was still capable of fighting. Yet even as he uttered the denial, he remembered the pitiful crew and passengers below. He remembered the mad woman, who only weeks ago had been young and beautiful, he remembered those who had died and those who were near to death. He remembered Susan.

'Mr Archibald!' he called to the signal midshipman, and was glad for the temporary relief when Travers told him that the young man was delivering a message below. 'Let him report to me when he returns.'

There was no immediate urgency, for the two French ships were still astern. It would be later, when the grabs and gallivats had slowed *Seahawk* to a bare two knots, that they would draw alongside and, if necessary, destroy *Seahawk* at their will.

'*Normandie*'s opened fire, sir!'

'What!' He couldn't believe that Lemarchand could think it necessary to waste a shot with her bow chaser.

'There, sir. She's firing her starboard guns,' Jones cried, 'though not at us.' He hesitated, as startled and unbelieving as Kelso at his side. 'Great heavens, sir, it's not us they're attacking. They're firing at the Mahrattans!'

21

'You were a worthy opponent, commodore,' Lemarchand said. 'I am almost sorry that our war is over.'

'Our *private* war,' Kelso replied, with a smile, 'for unless the dispatches from London lie hostilities continue in Europe and the Americas.'

Lemarchand shrugged and leant across to refill Kelso's glass with wine. 'Who knows what our governments decide to do in the west? In India it is we who decide, you and I, and I am pleased that we have been able to settle our differences like gentlemen.'

They were seated in some comfort in the huge round-house on the French ship of the line. After the Mahrattan grabs and gallivats had given up the fight, which they did with some alacrity when they saw that their erstwhile allies had changed sides, *Normandie*, flying a flag of truce, had sailed alongside, and through a speaking trumpet Lemarchand had invited Kelso aboard.

'Don't go!' Susan had urged, fearing a trick, and he remembered with affection the real concern she had shown.

'They have saved our ship, possibly our lives,' he had reminded. 'The least I can do is to appear civil.'

He had taken a liking to Lemarchand at once, recognizing in the elegant Frenchman a spirit kindred to his own. Here was a man, he thought, who liked honesty and, however hard he might fight, would show magnitude, even compassion, to a worthy opponent. Was this the reason which had persuaded him to change sides?

'When Pondicherry fell,' Lemarchand explained, 'and we were left with no secure base in India it seemed a good idea to form an alliance with the natural enemies of England, the Mahrattans.'

'I understand that,' Kelso replied, 'but if you will forgive my saying so, it was a strange alliance.'

'In what way?'

'The most civilized nation in Europe fighting alongside the barbarians.'

Lemarchand smiled and inclined his head, acknowledging the compliment. 'War makes strange bedfellows, as you well know. If we could form an alliance with Chandra Nath – '

'Chandra Nath?'

The Frenchman hesitated. 'Yes. You must have realized that although the government in Poona disowned the Gherians it was giving them every encouragement.'

'I had supposed so.'

'And that when Chandra Nath bargained with you on behalf of Kishun Roy he was in fact bargaining for himself.'

'I had guessed that, too,' Kelso said, dryly.

'If we could form an alliance with Chandra Nath, whose pirates were already causing you some embarrassment off Malabar, we could strike a blow against England and might eventually – for this was out real aim – help to drive you from Bombay.'

'That is Chandra Nath's intention still,' Kelso said. 'Of that I am sure. He still thinks he can succeed.'

'And you?'

Kelso looked at him for a moment before replying. It was pleasantly cool in the round house, with the ports open and a breeze tempering the shafts of sunlight that formed patterns on the deck. The steady creak of deck timbers as the ship rode, hove-to, with backed topsails, and the familiar harp of wind in the rigging had a pleasant, almost soporific effect on Kelso, who had slept only an hour last night and not much more the night before. Was it the wine or the unexpected sense of security which filled him with such a feeling of well being?

'I think Chandra Nath is seeking the courage to attack us. His aim is clearly to drive us from Bombay. For a long time he has hesitated, thinking, no doubt, that if he attacks and loses he will have lost everything, for there are other tribes who would be quick to take advantage of his discomfiture.'

'The Afghans, for instance?'

'Certainly. They are stronger than the Mahrattans, in my opinion, and better fighters. They only need an excuse.'

'But until the Afghans attack – *if* they attack.' Lemarchand continued, 'what prospects for the British?'

Kelso smiled as he took up his glass of wine and drank. 'I was just thinking that the government in London would be horrified to hear us talking like this, but you have done me the honour of being frank and I can only be frank in exchange.' He looked down at his glass as he chose his words.

'My honest opinion, although I'll tell you fairly that it's not shared by all my colleagues, is that whatever Chandra Nath sends against us we shall survive. We shall be out numbered and out-gunned, of course, we shall be fighting on or before an island from which there can be no retreat; but numbers are not everything, as we – and you – have proved often enough.

'I was with Robert Clive at Plassey, I was with him at the earlier attack on Gheriah. Steadfast fighters and determined leaders can make nonsense of the odds. I hope the Mahrattans don't attack, but if they do I, for one, shall have no thought of surrender.'

Lemarchand, who had been watching him keenly as he spoke, nodded and smiled. 'You are a man after my own heart, commodore. I almost wish I could be here fighting with you.'

Kelso returned the smile. 'Perhaps it won't come to that.'

'Not when Chandra Nath learns of your attack on Gheriah? Not when he knows that he has lost his prisoners?'

'He'll be upset, of course, but we still have to see whether he has the resolution.'

Through the open port he could see the topmasts and rigging of *Seahawk* as she moved gently to the swell. *Rouen* was to windward, guarding against any Mahrattan counter-attack, although the grabs and gallivats had long since disappeared over the horizon.

'I expect you are wondering,' Lemarchand said, 'why I decided to change sides.'

'I think I know.'

Lemarchand looked at him in surprise. 'I wonder.'

'You formed an alliance with the Mahrattans because it seemed to be in the best interests of France. You could harass the English, even though you had lost your last base in India, and you might even drive us from Bombay. You had everything to gain and nothing to lose – or so it seemed.'

Lemarchand nodded. 'So it seemed.'

'But you had not been reckoning on civilians, men, women and children, being used as hostages. When *Cleopatra* was taken you realized, perhaps for the first time, the true nature of your allies. You saw them not as splendid seamen, fanatical if bloodthirsty warriors, but, quite simply, as barbarians, men who would show no compassion to their prisoners, men who would rape or torture or kill at a whim. You realized, my dear Lemarchand, because you are a gentleman, that whatever material success you might achieve, an alliance with these barbarians could only harm the name of France.'

For a long time the Frenchman was silent. The ship's bell on *Seahawk* sounded faintly across the water and was answered almost immediately by the bell overhead. There was the sound of footsteps on the companion and on the quarterdeck and a mumble of voices that marked the change of watch.

'You saw them,' Lemarchand said, in a low voice, 'and that is perhaps the main reason I had to see you. Don't blame me, commodore, or not entirely, for what you saw. I tried, sometimes, I believe, to the extent of risking my own safety, but Kishun Roy was adamant. The English were his enemies, the English must suffer. Once, when he knew that his own brother had been killed, it was all I could do to stop him slaughtering them on the spot. He is an animal, Kelso, a dangerous beast, and when you made your daring rescue this morning I knew what I must do.'

'Well, I can only thank you,' Kelso said, 'for without your help we should all have been killed – or worse.'

The Frenchman raised his hand, disclaiming the need for thanks, and said, 'I tell you this, though: when we knew that you were coming and even when you so astutely altered the point of attack, I would not have given a fig for your chances – of reaching the prison even, let alone setting the prisoners free.'

'Setting them free was easy,' Kelso said, 'getting them to the beach was the problem. If we could have moved faster, if two had not died on the journey, if one poor soul had not lost her wits, we could have reached *Seahawk* by dawn and blocked the channel as we intended. But we were too late, the gallivats were already clear. All we could do was make all sail and run before the wind.'

Lemarchand stood up and looked out to the sea and

sky. 'You will want to be on your way, commodore. I can only wish you God speed. I hope that we shall meet again some day, under different circumstances.'

'I hope so too. Now you will return to France?'

'With all speed. I wish I could be sure of the reception I shall receive, but I believe I have done my duty by France.'

'You have done the best you can, following the dictates of your conscience,' Kelso said. 'No one could do more.'

'I hope the government in Paris sees it that way.'

As they came out on deck the sun welcomed them like an old friend. The air was warm, but not uncomfortably so, and the deck rocked comfortingly beneath their feet. On the bulwark, just beyond the entry port, a gull watched them with predatory eyes.

'You say you knew that we were coming?' Kelso asked. 'Is that why there were so few Mahrattans at the prison?'

'Of course. If you will allow me to say so, that was a brilliant stroke. All the Mahrattan forces were round the beach.'

'At Kalewa?'

'Yes. That's where we were told you would land.'

Kelso looked across the water to *Seahawk* where Jones, anticipating his arrival, had the piper waiting. Travers was there, too, and Lovegrove, the bo'sun, while in the waist a few of the released prisoners were enjoying their first taste of freedom. Alone, by the weather rail, Susan waited.

'You knew of our plans, then?' Kelso asked. 'And, earlier, that's how you captured *Cleopatra*?'

'Of course.'

'And how you came to intercept us a few days ago?'

'Yes, I thought you knew.'

Kelso smiled grimly. 'I didn't know, but I guessed.'

'My dear commodore, I'm sorry to leave on a sour note, but I think you should know. Yes, Chandra Nath has a spy in your camp. He's known all your plans from the first.'

22

They made love with abandon, locked in each other's arms, bodies pressed hungrily together, almost as though they feared it might be for the last time. Afterwards they lay side by side, fingers intertwined and watched dawn come up over the distant mountains. It was cool, or as cool as it was likely to get at this time of year, and they lay silently, content with each other's presence, while a dog barked and a door opened and shut as the bhisti made his early morning trip to the well and a cock in a neighbouring garden crowed for the third time.

'I must go.' He kissed her lightly on the forehead as he rose from the bed and went into the shower.

'Shall you be long?'

'It depends. Richard Bouchier had called a council meeting. There's a fair amount to decide.'

'About the poor souls from *Cleopatra*?'

'That certainly: and what reaction we're likely to get from Chandra Nath.'

'Do you think that he'll attack?'

'I wish I knew. Losing his French allies has obviously weakened his position, but like most of these potentates he's a vindictive man.'

He came naked from the shower, rubbing his body with a towel, and looked down at her. 'Why not come with me?'

'To the council meeting?'

'Not to the meeting, but to town. It's a long time since we walked out together.'

She hesitated only a moment before pushing herself from the pillows. 'That would be nice. While you're deciding the fate of India I'll call on Caroline Bouchier.'

'She'll be surprised to see you so early.'

'I doubt that she'll be up, for she seldom rises before noon. No wonder she's getting fat!'

They walked out by the cliff path, which brought back memories of their arrival in Bombay nine years ago when she had been a young widow, not thinking of a second marriage, much less a third, while he had been a Company officer, just twenty-one yet expecting his first command. How much had happened since then!

He took her hand as they crossed a ditch and came out on a headland overlooking the sea. It was his favourite view, with the whole island below and, to their right, the bay curving to the measureless limits of sky and sea.

'Careful!' She pulled at his hand, for he had brought her to a precipice edge. Below, *Seahawk* was taking on provisions, ready for the next voyage while *Malabar*, which had returned from patrol, *Cleopatra* and the two bomb ketches were anchored in deep water.

'There she is,' he said, pointing to *Cleopatra*. 'I'd give a lot to know what happened aboard her before she was captured.'

'Don't you know?' She looked at him uncertainly. 'I thought you had questioned everyone.'

'Not Tulliver, poor devil, who's dead, nor Fenton.' He was silent for a moment and then said, 'It's strange that Fenton should have been so mysterious. He *knew* something was wrong; of that I'm convinced, yet he didn't want to put it on paper.'

'Well, you'll soon find out, for *Protector* should be in with the new convoy before long.'

'I hope so.'

She looked at him curiously. 'I hadn't thought about

it, for I understood your enquiries were over, but it occurs to me that *Cleopatra*'s officers, or those that are alive, are below. Couldn't you question them?'

'I intend to.'

'And the passengers? perhaps they know something.'

'They were below, or should have been, as soon as Abercrombie gave the order to clear for action.'

'Not Ralph Pettigrew. Have you asked him?'

He looked at her guardedly. 'Yes. I've asked him, but let me get this clear: are you saying that while *Cleopatra* was preparing for action Pettigrew was on deck?'

'Yes. I heard him asking the captain, and stressing his position as ex-member of council when Abercrombie demurred.'

'So he stayed there – for how long?'

'I'm not sure. I was in the cockpit, seeing if I could help. Sir Ralph came down some time later.'

'After poor Abercrombie had been brought below?'

'Yes, I think so. To be honest I was so upset – ' She hesitated and then said, with conviction, 'Yes, it was afterwards. I remember I came out of the cockpit, feeling that I must have some air, and I stumbled into him as he came down the companion.' She held his arm tightly, for they were still on the cliff edge and asked, 'Didn't Sir Ralph tell you this himself?'

'He told me that he stayed on deck, but only for a few minutes.'

They were coming down towards the town now on a path which led across an area of scrubland. Flowering bushes, yellow, purple and scarlet, flaunted their colours and filled the air with scent. A host of cicadas chirruped gaily in the grass.

'One more question.' He stopped and turned to face her. 'What was the relationship between Kishun Roy and his brother?'

'They were devoted. Kishun is a hard, ruthless man: his one weakness, I felt, was his brother Bedi.'

He looked down into her grey eyes, which were watching him calmly but with a faint hint of perlexity.

'Good!' He nodded, without explanation, and suddenly, to her great surprise, soundly kissed her.

The members of council were all assembled as he reached the governor's residence, and Pettigrew was waiting for him in the ante-room. 'Kelso, you're late, damme! The governor is getting impatient.'

'Then we'd best go in.'

They all rose as he entered, Sir Ralph, at the head of the table, Raikes and Emmerson and a sickly looking Carew. 'Come, gentlemen,' the governor said. 'Sit down, for there's much to consider.'

When Kelso and Pettigrew had taken their places, facing each other across the table, the governor said, 'First, Kelso, I think we should all like to set on record our appreciation and thanks for what was yet another remarkable achievement. How you managed with just one frigate, and that not fully seaworthy, and – '

'Thank you, sir,' Kelso interrupted. 'I am grateful for your kind words.' He looked round. 'Please don't think me ungracious, gentlemen, but may I suggest that with so many pressing problems we should pass on to more urgent matters?'

'Oh, very well.' The governor looked slightly discomfited, but Pettigrew laughed. 'Always the same Kelso – never one for testimonials!'

'Not while the safety of every Englishman in Bombay is in jeopardy,' Kelso replied. 'Am I right in assuming, sir,' he asked, turning to the governor, 'that you have had an ultimatum from Chandra Nath?'

'I have it here.' The governor opened a double sheet of parchment and spread it on the table. 'It is an ultimatum, as you say. Chandra Nath reminds us that he indicated clearly to you, Kelso and Pettigrew, the consequences should we take it upon ourselves to attack Gheriah.'

'We haven't attacked it,' Kelso pointed out. 'We merely called to free some Britons who had been abducted and were being abominably treated by the Gherians over whom, he says, he has no control.'

'Well, that's as maybe, but it's not the way he sees it.'

'What is this ultimatum?'

The governor pursed his lips. 'He's raised his price, as we expected. He now wants ten crores, delivered to him within a week or an undertaking in writing that we will quit Bombay.'

Kelso nodded. 'I wonder which he'd prefer.'

'Whichever it is,' Raikes protested, 'it's quite unacceptable.'

'That goes without saying. The question is, what shall we do?'

'What *can* we do?' the governor asked, 'except wait? We'll put troops on instant alert, of course, and take another look at our defences. But if the Mahrattans do attack – and I understand from our intelligence in Poona that they are mobilizing – we shall have to fight. The odds will be against us, at something like a hundred to one, but we have the advantage of a narrow front and now, thank goodness, since the French have withdrawn, command of the seas.'

'One must hope so,' Pettigrew added, 'although I'm sure Kelso won't take it amiss when I say that there's no certainty about it. Two frigates, a less than seaworthy sloop and the bomb ketches are hardly a convincing defence against an untold number of grabs and gallivats.'

'Pettigrew's right,' Kelso said, 'although I am not without confidence. In any case, can he suggest what else we should do?'

'Yes.' Pettigrew leant forward and looked round the table. 'If we want to stay in Bombay, even more if we value the lives of Britons living here, we should meet Chandra Nath's demands.'

'Pay his ransom, you mean?' Raikes cried. 'You must be mad!'

'Not mad, but realistic. It's our only chance.'

'Where would we find that enormous sum of money?'

'By borrowing, if necessary, by calling on Madras and Calcutta for help.'

'Within a week?'

'We can temporize. Chandra Nath won't be too impatient if we send him even a token payment as a sign of good faith.'

'How much do you suggest?' Kelso asked, quietly.

'How much? As much as we can raise – two crores, even one.'

'Only a fraction of what he asks,' Kelso commented, 'but still a huge sum of money.' He looked across the table. 'And I suppose your share would be considerable.'

'My what?' Pettigrew could not have been more surprised if Kelso had leant across and struck him. His cheeks drained of colour and his eyes widened with fear or apprehension. 'What the devil do you mean?'

'Let's drop the pretences,' Kelso said. 'It's taken me a long time to fix the traitor – too long, for I should have realized long ago that it was you.'

'Have a care!' Pettigrew said, pushing back his chair. 'Don't forget I have witnesses. I'm not afraid to call you out.'

'I've known there was a traitor from the first,' Kelso said, 'and I've suspected everyone, all of you in this room, my steward Padstow, although I could hardly believe that he would have the knowledge or the means. I've even suspected my own wife.'

'And why not?' Pettigrew cried, savagely. 'Wasn't she the one passenger given special privileges in Gheriah?'

'Apart from yourself.'

'But she was living with Bedi Roy, Kishun's brother: did you know that? She shared his apartment. It's Calcutta all over again – and don't think I don't know what happened there. Do you think that Kishun Roy didn't know you had landed on your first attempt? You were seen rowing ashore and word was in Gheriah almost before you had landed. Didn't you know that your wife's escape was planned?'

'I think it was planned all right,' Kelso said, 'but not in the way you suggest. It puzzled me at the time that you, a prisoner of the Mahrattans, should be aware that we had landed at Kalewa. Why should the Mahrattans tell you? It also occurred to me that the Mahrattan pursuit was almost perfunctory – a few soldiers jogging behind us, a hundred yards to the rear. They even conveniently kept running when we left the track.'

'So, the Mahrattans allowed us to escape,' Pettigrew cried, at least, they allowed Lady Susan to escape.'

'No,' Kelso said. 'I considered that at first – to my shame – but I realize now that I was wrong. If Kishun Roy was willing to let us escape so that he could have his spy in the English camp it wasn't Susan he was helping: it was you.'

'Why me? Why not your wife?'

'Kishun was fond of his brother. He would never have agreed to the killing of Bedi.' He looked at Pettigrew without mercy. 'You forget that it was Susan who killed his brother.'

Pettigrew licked his lips and looked wildly from one to another, seeing no help or forgiveness in their astonished but angry expressions.

'My suspicions were first aroused,' Kelso said, 'when I

heard of *Cleopatra*'s capture. How had the French and the Mahrattans caught up with her? It wasn't until I pressed you that I found out about the faulty steering, for it wasn't in your report to the governor.'

'It didn't seem important.'

'Not important, when it allowed the Mahrattans to capture *Cleopatra* and take those poor souls – the lucky ones who are little better than living skeletons and those others who went mad or died! Kelso leant across the table and his fists were clenched as he asked, 'Did you think of that, Pettigrew, when you tampered with the steering chains?'

'Why should I do that?' Pettigrew asked, despairingly, for his expression and his wild, hopeful glances from one member of council to another were enough to proclaim his guilt.

'Why, indeed!' Kelso said. 'And why did you have to kill poor Abercrombie, unless it was because he realized, too late, that it was you who had succeeded in delaying his ship?'

'It's not true! I was below.'

'Not when Abercrombie was killed. Susan confirms that, and only yesterday I spoke to one of the prisoners from Gheriah, a certain Midshipman Goodchild, who remembers you standing aft with Abercrombie – arguing, he thought, although his attention was soon diverted when *Normandie* opened fire.'

'Lies! Lies! It's all lies!' Pettigrew cried.

'The evidence continued to build up,' Kelso said. 'For instance, why did you have to go with me to Poona? To get fresh orders from Chandra Nath? And how did Chandra Nath know that Carew and Forster were sick?'

'There are spies everywhere,' Pettigrew cried. 'You know that. Every khitmutgar or punkah wallah hears things which he'll pass on for a price.'

'Not these things,' Kelso said. 'It had to be someone in this room.'

'And that's what you believe?'

'How were *Normandie* and *Rouen* able to intercept us on our second expedition?' Kelso asked. 'That was really the last straw.'

There was a silence until the governor, who like his fellow members, had been listening to this with growing indignation and astonishment, said, 'If your suspicions were so overwhelming, Kelso, why didn't you do something? Why not denounce Pettigrew before this last expedition?'

Kelso looked hard at Pettigrew before he replied. 'Because I had no positive proof, also I saw how I could get the traitor to help us, while bringing about his own undoing.'

'You mean, on the last expedition?'

'I told you all that we would anchor in the lee of the headland at Gheriah and that we would send out landing party ashore at Kalewa. The ruse worked better than I expected. While we continued south to the other side of the channel the Mahrattans had their forces waiting around Kalewa. It meant that there was only a handful of troops guarding the prison and that we were able to make our slow way back to the beach.' He cried angrily across the table, 'I wonder how you'll explain that, Pettigrew, to your Mahrattan masters!'

'It's not true!' Pettigrew beat his hands on the table. 'Not true!' His face was suddenly old and ugly, and he looked near to tears. 'You're determined to bring me down,' he added. 'God knows why, but you admit yourself, you've no proof.'

'Not until two days ago,' Kelso said. 'Not until Lemarchand decided to change sides. You couldn't have foreseen that.'

'Lemarchand, the French commander!' Pettigrew stared at him in disbelief. 'But he couldn't – ' He stopped.

'Couldn't have known? Is that what you were going to say? Well, you're wrong. Whatever promises Chandra Nath made to you didn't stop him telling his French ally.'

'I don't believe it!'

'The last thing Lemarchand told me when I left his ship was that we had a traitor in the camp. He asked if I knew who it was and I said I had my suspicions. Then he smiled and wrote something on a slip of paper and sealed it in an envelope. 'There,' he said. 'Open it when you get to Bombay and see if your suspicions are correct.' Kelso took out an envelope and laid it on the table. 'This envelope,' he said to Pettigrew. 'Do you want me to open it?'

There was a long silence while Pettigrew seemed to shrink lower and lower into his chair. His eyes, fixed on the envelope, were mad and staring, his mouth hung loosely open. Overhead the punkah continued its monotonous flapping.

'It's India you should be blaming,' Pettigrew said at last, speaking more to himself than to his audience, 'not me. I came here as a young man, just a boy really, believing that I'd make a fortune by thirty and return home to live the life of a sahib.

'Things went well at first. I was not without influence, nor did I lack connections, for my uncle, Sir Basil, was a member of council at Fort William. It was through him that I was granted the lease of salt farms at Haranish.'

'Which you sublet to some wretched Armenian and then reneged on your agreement,' Kelso said. 'Don't think your past misdeeds can excuse you.'

'I only did what other Englishmen were doing,' Pettigrew flared. 'We all had the same aim – to make money quickly, by whatever means, and return home. Why should I be singled out?'

'Because everyone was not like you. There were honest men, like John Holwell and others, who worked hard to advance the Company's interests.'

'Aye, and left India, if they left it at all, with nothing but ill health for their pains.'

'And their good names,' the governor added. 'They returned as they came, honourable men.'

Pettigrew made a derisive sweep with his arm. 'Honourable men! Honourable fools! Are you telling me that those of us who have suffered the climate, the flies, the dust and the diseases of this benighted country don't deserve some reward?' He looked round aggressively and, receiving no reply, went on, 'I was determined to return home rich; I'll not deny it. When I lost one fortune, through no fault of my own – '

'At the gaming table,' Kelso reminded.

'All right! At cards. Don't a man need some relaxation?' He simmered for a while on his self pity, and then went on. 'I made another fortune when Mir Jaffir was persuaded to recompense the English merchants after Plassey.'

'Although you lost nothing,' Kelso said, 'because you had nothing to lose. It was unfortunate that Mir Jaffir was not sure enough of his position to resist.'

'Why should he resist when he had vaults stacked with gold and precious stones, and he knew that without the British he would be Surajah Dowlah's servant or worse?'

Kelso looked at him across the table and said, without anger, 'There is such a thing as justice.'

'Justice! What has life in India to do with justice? It was a rotten, stinking, corrupt country long before the British came. If we, by our skills and superior intelligence, beat the natives at their own game isn't that to our credit? It's men like you, Kelso, and you, Sir Richard, judging people on the standards of Europe, who are unjust. We take what we can, within the customs of the country, and if we are fortunate enough to go home rich we are applauded and given the title of nabob: but if, like me, we lose everything we are called traitors and pariahs: is that it?'

'So you lost your second fortune,' the governor said. 'Are you saying that it was not your fault?'

'Of course it wasn't my fault,' Pettigrew said, almost spitting the words across the table. 'Ask Kelso here. Ask him how I lost it. Let him tell you how I and other unfortunates were outwitted by a woman.'

It was the point Kelso had been dreading, but now that it had come he knew that he must face it. He wondered what Susan was doing now and pictured her, cool and aristocratic as ever, taking coffee with the governor's lady. Was there anything, except the incalculable gift of judgment, to separate her conduct from Pettigrew's?

'I imagine you are referring to your business ventures in Calcutta,' Kelso said, 'ventures which were speculative to say the least. You lost your fortune by bad judgment and – I'll give you this – bad luck. It's stupid and vindictive to blame Susan for being more successful.'

'Yes, but how, and why, that's what you should ask. How could your precious Susan find goods to sell – European goods – when the convoy was two months overdue? How did she gain the betel concession, the most valued in Bengal? How did she corner the wine market and by forcing up prices as high as she dared make yet another fortune above the ones she already had?'

Kelso did not reply, for he could not without betraying Susan. Most of what Pettigrew had said was true, and it was for this that he had ordered Susan to England. Now, all that was over – or so he had thought. It was the governor who came to his rescue.

'How Lady Susan made her fortune is neither here nor there, although I've known her as long as you, Pettigrew, and I'll wager that it was by hard work and energy and perhaps a divine womanly instinct that she gained the advantage over others like you. But that don't signify. What matters now is that you have been guilty of a crime far worse than mere greed or envy: you are guilty of treason.'

'Aye, and because of you good men and women have lost their lives,' Raikes accused, 'and others have suffered unspeakable pain and hardship. That's what you've to answer for, Pettigrew, not greed or dishonesty or peculation. You've sinned against your own kind.'

The governor nodded. 'And against that there is no defence.' He looked down at the table, considering. 'You must consider yourself under arrest. By rights I should ask Colonel Ashton to have you put under guard. But I'll not do that, for the sake of your family and for the memory of your father, whom I knew well. If you will give me your word that you'll not leave Bombay or even your house without my permission I'll let you go, unescorted. Do you agree?'

Pettigrew looked round the table and there was such a degree of malice in his eyes that everyone felt uneasy. 'On my honour – is that it?' He laughed shortly. 'So be it. You have my word.' He rose abruptly, knocking over his glass of wine, and hurried from the room.

The governor sighed. 'What a tragedy, the more so because he comes of good stock! I knew his father well, and his mother, God rest her soul, was the gentlest of women.'

'He killed Abercrombie,' Raikes reminded, 'and those others who died under the Mahrattans. He arranged the capture of *Cleopatra* and all her cargo. He has put the lives of everyone – every Englishman – in Bombay in danger. Don't look to me for pity.'

'Aye, you're right,' the governor acknowledged, 'although I can't help thinking there's something in what he said.'

'What was that?' Kelso asked, sharply.

'Why, that India is partly to blame: this India we love and hate and defend against all the odds must bear some responsibility.' He reached across and took the envelope which still lay on the table. 'I suppose I'd better open this, although I doubt that we can use it as evidence.'

He broke the seal and looked inside. Then, with a startled expression, he looked across at Kelso. 'It's empty,' he said.

'Of course.' Kelso said, in a level tone, 'Lemarchand confirmed that there was a traitor although he didn't know his name. The envelope was my idea.'

23

The convoy from England, escorted by *Protector*, had sailed in on the morning tide and now lay at anchor in the bay. Passengers had come ashore, cargo was being unloaded, and arms and victualling parties were already taking fresh supplies aboard. In a few days, a week at the most, the bluff-bowed Indiamen would continue their voyage to Comorin and round the cape to Madras. Fenton, after reporting to the governor, had accompanied Kelso up the hill to the house on the bluffs.

'I was sorry to hear about Pettigrew,' Fenton said, as they settled with a decanter of wine on the verandah. Below stretched a garden which was reluctantly responding to Susan's determined assault and was actually boasting a few sickly looking roses among the flamboyants. The lawn, too, was green in patches where the bhisti, again on Susan's instructions, had been persuaded to bring goatskins of water from the well. Beyond, a more familiar and restful background to both, stretched the sea.

'You suspected him from the first?' Kelso asked.

'Not really, although I gathered from *Cleopatra*'s erratic behaviour and from what Abercrombie told me that there might be a renegade aboard.'

'But you had no reason to suspect Pettigrew?'

'Well –' Fenton hesitated and, to cover his confusion, took a hasty sip of wine.

'You saw him in Madras when you went ashore, isn't that the truth? You saw him with Susan.' Kelso looked keenly at his friend, and then added with a smile, 'Susan wasn't implicated in any way. I know that now, so you can be honest.'

'I wasn't thinking of Susan at all,' Fenton lied, and then, failing to meet Kelso's eye, blushed. 'I mean, she was with Pettigrew in one of the markets, I couldn't help seeing them. An Indian came up and accosted them, or perhaps it was only Pettigrew he wanted. In any case they went off together.'

'All three?'

'Yes, although later, when I was in the fruit market, I saw Susan again.'

'Still with Pettigrew and the Indian?'

'No. She was alone. At least, she was following some-one, or so I thought, and although I only caught a glimpse it seemed to be your steward Padstow.'

Kelso nodded and smiled. 'That's right. Padstow told me. She helped him to buy some fruit.'

Fenton drained his glass and did not protest as Kelso leant across to refill it. He seemed relieved. 'So Pettigrew had gone off with Chandra Nath's messenger?'

'It's probable. I thought it strange that Susan returned to *Cleopatra* alone.'

Fenton was silent for a moment and then, perhaps emboldened by the wine, said, 'If you'll forgive me saying so I'm delighted – more than delighted – that Lady Susan has decided to stay.'

'Thank you.' Kelso said, quietly, 'We've had our differences. I can say that to you as an old friend, but we'll never be happy apart. I know that now, and I'm grateful that she's returned.'

'She's a remarkable woman,' Fenton said, sincerely.

A platoon of the Thirty-ninth Foot were marching up the road, their red jackets already white with dust. A supply wagon drawn by oxen was moving slowly in the same direction towards the forward defences on the isthmus, from where, in a moment, a gun boomed.

'Only a ranging shot,' Kelso said, as Fenton started. 'We'll know soon enough when the Mahrattans appear – at least I hope so. There are patrols out along the road, and *Agamemnon* and *Seahawk* are on sea watch.'

'You think Chandra Nath will attack?'

'I think he must now that he's committed himself so far. According to intelligence he's mobilized an army of a hundred thousand in the hills. The Mahrattan soldiers are doubtless feeling that they've had peace too long. Even Chandra Nath would have difficulty in persuading them to lay down arms now.'

'And you think that Bombay can survive?'

Kelso hesitated and then spoke slowly, choosing his words with care. 'I think the chances are even, although on paper we should be swept into the sea. On land we shall be defending a narrow front with soldiers who, thanks to Ashton, are disciplined and well trained. At sea we shall be fighting a horde of grabs and gallivats, which we have met often enough in the past, as you know well, so we shall know what to expect. When Robert Clive was here we accepted odds like these without a thought. As I see it there is no reason why we should be less confident today.' He took a sip of wine and added, 'In any case, it had to come sooner or later. For my part, I would sooner meet the Mahrattans now, when we are ready, than wait a year or more in suspense.'

Again the gun boomed and a few pigeons flew into the air.

'I've always mistrusted the Mahrattans,' Fenton confessed, 'although I've never hated them until now.'

'Because of what they did to *Cleopatra*'s passengers and crew?'

'That certainly.' He turned to Kelso and said, 'You

191

know, sir, I still wonder whether I was right to continue with the rest of the convoy. I couldn't believe that even the Mahrattans could be such barbarians. Was I right to act as I did – I hope, sir, you'll be honest – or should I have turned before the wind and given chase?'

'You did what I would have done,' Kelso replied, 'what any responsible commander would have done. Don't blame yourself. You had no choice.'

'Thank you, sir.'

'But I agree with you about the Mahrattans. If you had seen the condition of the wretched prisoners we found in Gheriah you would probably be even more incensed. And what they did to Pettigrew – you've heard about that?' He shook his head. 'The man was a traitor and would have been shot in any case if he hadn't broken his parole: but to die like that – !'

Pettigrew had ridden out the same evening, breaking his pledge to the governor and making, according to the forward posts which let him pass, for Poona. Whether he expected to find help and sympathy from Chandra Nath they would never know, for he returned two days later as a mutilated corpse tied to the saddle of his horse. It was then that the forces in Bombay had gone on full alert.

'What do you want me to do, sir?' Fenton asked. 'The Indiamen below are quite capable of giving a good account of themselves, but I doubt that they'd stand much chance against so many grabs and gallivats.'

'They must stay here, for a few days at least. In the meantime *Protector* will add to our defences.'

Fenton nodded. 'How long, do you think, before they attack?'

'I wish I knew. They'll come in at dawn, I expect, or late at night. I'm only surprised they haven't come already.'

'Perhaps Chandra Nath is getting cold feet.'

'I doubt it.'

He turned as from the corner of his eye he caught a movement on the road. Padstow was trudging up the hill, red-faced, perspiring freely, and pausing every few minutes to exchange pleasantries with the following swarm of flies. Ten minutes passed before he climbed the last two or three hundred yards, but instead of going indoors he came round to the verandah and saluted.

''Morning, sir,' he said, to Fenton. 'The commodore'll be glad to see you've brought *Protector* back safe and sound.'

'What is it?' Kelso asked.

'Message from the governor, sir. Could he have the pleasure of your company – yours too, sir,' he added, looking at Fenton.

'Are you sure? We've just come from there.'

'Something's happened, sir, or so I understand, something you ought to know about.'

'Very well.'

'Good news, sir, or so I gather,' Padstow remarked as he turned to go.

Kelso stood up. 'Padstow!'

'Sir?'

'What good news? You've obviously heard.'

'Don't rightly know, sir,' Padstow replied, putting on his blank expression, 'seein' as the governor don't confide in me.'

'Padstow!'

'Well, sir, I did hear – mind you, I may have got it wrong – I did hear that the Mahrattans are on the march.'

Kelso and Fenton exchnaged glances. 'And you call that good news?'

'Northwards, sir, or so I understand. It seems that another lot of barbarians – the Afghans would it be? – are making warlike noises on the border.'

Kelso nodded lest he should betray by his voice the relief he felt. 'Very well, Padstow. Thank you.'

'Don't thank me, sir. If you'd of asked me I'd 'ave preferred a good fight.'

As soon as the steward had left Kelso allowed himself a smile. 'Good news, Fenton. Our Afghan friends have responded at the right time.'

'It's wonderful news, sir.'

'Here!' Kelso picked up the decanter and filled their glasses. 'Let's drink to it.'

The sun was shining as they walked down the hill, but a sea breeze kept the air fresh and discouraged the flies which usually made walking at this time of day a test of endurance. The bougainvillaea was out, and lower down, by the creek, which still showed a few inches of muddy water, oleanders were blooming. A small boy playing in the dust held out his hand, more from habit than hope, and was taken aback when Kelso threw him a coin. A sergeant, looking hot and uncomfortable in his scarlet jacket, tight blue trousers and belt, clicked to attention and saluted.

'Carry on, sergeant.' Kelso could not remember when he had felt so happy.

Then he saw her.

She was coming out of the gown shop *Abigail Palmer's Emporium*, and she stopped and waved as they approached.

How lovely she is, Kelso thought, not smiling or returning her wave, but feeling nevertheless that her presence at this particular moment was almost more than he had a right to expect.

She greeted them coolly but with a graciousness that was all her own and said, 'Captain Fenton, I'm delighted to see you. I heard that *Protector* was safely returned. I do hope that you'll dine with us this evening.'

'Thank you, ma'am,' Fenton replied, blushing and looking, for all his six feet three inches, like an overgrown schoolboy. 'I would be honoured.'

194

'Seven o'clock then.' She smiled and added, 'I hope my husband won't insist on sea talk all the evening, for I'm longing to hear the latest gossip from St Helena.'

Fenton smiled and said, 'I'll do my best, ma'am.'

'What's the matter, dear?' Kelso asked, seeing that her hands were empty. 'Couldn't you find what you wanted? Come, let's go back again, for I'd like to buy you a present. Fenton and I will help you choose it.' He put his hand on his heart and said, with mock seriousness, 'And, as Fenton is your witness, I promise that whatever the cost I won't object.'

She looked at him thoughtfully for a moment, obviously wondering what had put him in this good humour. 'Very well, dear. That is most kind.'

She hesitated. 'The truth is, though, that it wasn't a dress I was wanting so much as a business venture. But now you're here, you and Captain Fenton, you can help me decide.' She smiled. 'I was thinking of buying the shop.'